हिमाली अपहरण

HIMALAYAN KIDNAP

THE FIRST ALEX AND JAMES
ECO–ADVENTURE IN NEPAL

Emerson

Printed in the United States of America

Published by Eifrig Publishing,
PO Box 66, Lemont, PA 16851,
Knobelsdorffstr. 44, 14059 Berlin, Germany

For information regarding permission, write to:
Rights and Permissions Department,
Eifrig Publishing, LLC
PO Box 66, Lemont, PA 16851, USA.
permissions@eifrigpublishing.com, 888-340-6543.

Library of Congress Cataloging-in-Publication Data

Wilson-Howarth, Jane
Himalayan Kidnap
/ written by Jane Wilson-Howarth, illustrated by Betty Levene

    p.   cm.

Paperback: ISBN 978-1-63233-100-7
Hardcover: ISBN 978-1-63233-101-4
Ebook: ISBN 978-1-63233-102-1

1. Juvenile Fiction-Adventure. 2. Juvenile Fiction-Nepal
I. Wilson-Howarth, Jane II. Title.

21 20 19 18 17 2016
5 4 3 2 1

Printed on acid-free paper. ∞

हिमाली अपहरण

HIMALAYAN KIDNAP

THE FIRST ALEX AND JAMES ECO—ADVENTURE IN NEPAL

JANE WILSON—HOWARTH
ILLUSTRATIONS BY BETTY LEVENE

Eifrig Publishing LLC
Lemont Berlin

This book is dedicated to everyone who works to help impoverished people (particularly in the aftermath of the 2015 earthquakes) and to those who strive to protect Nepal's threatened wildlife.

J.W.-H.

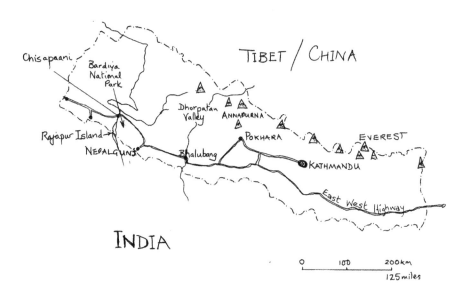

Nepali and other unfamiliar words are highlighted in the text with * and defined at the end of the book.

TABLE OF CONTENTS

"The spotted deer stag turned, showing off his fine antlers"

1
BLOOD–SUCKERS

No matter how often I shook my head, flies landed back on my face. Blinking didn't keep them out of my eyes either. They slurped stuff from the corners. They walked on my lips. Something bigger tickled the end of my nose. I looked cross-eyed. Two of them were mating on me. I tried to blow them away. They weren't bothered.

We didn't know why those men had picked on our family, why they'd made that phone call, which in a few short days had turned our lives into a complete nightmare. All we knew was they'd left us here, tied together around a thin tree.

A fly landed by my nostril. It actually went inside my nose—until I sort of snorted it out. This had to be a bad dream. I shook my head again. That felt real enough. Ropes cut into my wrists. This was no dream. If we didn't do something, we'd die here.

"Hey, James," I rasped.

"Huh?"

"You asleep?"

"I was till you woke me." He fidgeted and pulled the ropes so they hurt my wrists even more. "So what happens now, Alex?"

"I dunno."

"I want a drink," said James.

"Yeah. Me too." My voice was scratchy, my tongue thick. It stuck to the roof of my mouth.

James made a strange spluttering sound. "*Aggh,* a big fat fly just flew into my mouth! And ants are biting me again— they *really* hurt!"

"Try wriggling your butt about."

He yelped. "That's made them even angrier."

We were sitting on the dry dirt. Each of my hands was tied to my little brother's so our arms encircled the smooth tree-trunk. Roped like this with our backs to the tree, we couldn't even really look at each other.

"When will they come back, Alex?"

"I don't know. I don't suppose they care. Not now they've got the money."

Saying that out loud made me choke up. I was glad James couldn't see my face.

For a long time, I just sat. I had to face up to it, though. We were the only ones who could get ourselves out of this mess. And James wasn't going to see me fall apart. I pulled at our ropes. The kidnappers must have made them themselves— by twisting together vines or grass or something. They didn't look strong, but how they cut into my wrists! Moving was pointless; it just made James yelp.

"Look... I have an idea. Get the matches out of my pocket, will you?"

"Why?"

"Just do it, James."

"But why?"

"So I can burn through these ropes."

"That won't work."

"Yeah maybe but *try*, will you."

He shuffled around. He pulled. "Can't reach."

"You've got to. Try harder."

"I can't," he said.

"Oh come on!"

"I really can't."

There was a *kak kak* alarm shout from a langur in a tree above us. This was not a good sign. I edged my bottom towards James' left hand. "I'm closer. Try again."

I felt him wriggle. "It's no use. I really, really can't reach."

"I've moved a bit more. Try again. *Aggh*—those ants are evil!"

"Yeah—I *know*."

After lots and lots more struggling, James got his hand on my trousers, then the ends of his fingers into my pocket. He fumbled inside. Some coins fell out. He rummaged in my pocket and got fingers on either side of the matchbox. Finally, he pulled out a battered pack of matches. He dropped them. He scrabbled with his fingers and got them back into his hand. He took out a match. Then, with James striking the match and me holding the box, he lit one. He dropped that. It went out. We lit another. He managed to get it between two fingers and position it under one of the bits of rope holding our wrists. "Oi! Ow! You're burning *me*!"

"Oh. Can't see. Sorry." James didn't sound sorry.

My skin was stinging. I could smell matches and burning leaves. "Don't go starting a forest fire, now!"

Then James said, "What was that?"

"What was what?" I smelt burnt arm hair.

"That bark."

"Spotted deer. Alarm calls. Quite close."

"Yeah, yeah, but something's moving over there," he said jerking his chin towards the thickest patch of undergrowth. "Alarm barks—I don't like the sound of that. It could mean there's a leopard or tiger about."

"Nah. There aren't any man-eaters around here."

"Maybe, but it's like we've been left out as bait."

"Come on—just concentrate on the matches, will you?"

"Look. Something *is* moving—over there, Alex."

I scanned the undergrowth. Small leaves trembled like they were scared, too. Otherwise nothing stirred. "It's just the wind."

"Nah." James farted noisily. "*That's* wind."

"You're such a gentleman." Then James sighed with relief, "Ah, it's only a blood-sucker."

A couple of metres away, a chisel-toothed lizard, with bright orange head and shoulders had run out into the open and was doing push-ups.

"They're such show-offs."

He reared up as another blood-sucker burst out of the undergrowth and rushed at him. The two of them—both up on their hind legs now—pushed and shoved and struggled like wrestlers. The first one squirmed to get his mouth locked onto the other's side. There was blood. The bitten lizard broke free, ran and disappeared into the jungle*.

Sounds came from another part of the undergrowth. Surely other more dangerous creatures lurked there. Finally, I saw stealthy movement. It was more than one animal. But what? Cats hunt on their own; bears are loners, too. I don't know why I said it out loud, but I did. "At least big cats are kind killers."

"What do you mean *kind* killers, Alex?"

"Tigers bite you once in the neck and err—it's quick."

"That's reassuring!"

"Yeah, wild dogs aren't so nice. They disembowel their prey first—eat the guts—while they're still alive—and entrails become extrails...."

"Shut up!"

"Okay sorry, James. Maybe it's jungle fowl or peacocks or something?"

"Birds make more noise than that."

As if to call me a liar, a loud bird call close by started up. It startled me. The call seemed to be saying, "*brain fev-er, go cra-zy, brain fev-er, go cra-zy, brain fever, go crazy, brain fever, go crazy, brainfever, gocrazy, brainfevergocrazy, gocrazeey, gocrazeey, gocrazeey.*" The call got faster and faster, higher and higher in pitch, so that it sounded like the bird was completely trying to unhinge us.

I shook my head to drive the sounds away. I stared into the undergrowth until my eyes ached. Then I caught a glimpse of reddish-brown and a whiff of old dog. There was another blur of reddish fur. I saw a bushy tail and a wolf-like shape. It took me a few more seconds to be sure. "Indian wild dogs—a pack of them."

"Oh."

"It's okay. They don't attack people," I said, knowing they are really clever. I'd heard they kill the occasional tiger.

James said exactly what I was thinking. "Maybe they don't *usually* attack people, but people aren't *usually* trussed up like oven-ready turkeys—are they?"

"Keep working on those ropes, James," I said through clenched teeth. My wrists were *so* sore. "Light another match!"

There were more alarm-barks from the deer, but there were other sounds, much closer. Two wild dogs poked their heads out of the undergrowth. They lifted up their noses and sniffed the air. They were wolf-sized, long-legged and looked ferocious.

Their eyes were at our eye level. Their teeth were at the level of our faces. Saliva dripped from their mouths. We sat absolutely still. They stared at us for ages. I wanted to swallow but dared not. There was a yelp from another of the pack and they ran towards that sound: away from us. The barks from the deer became more urgent, panicky. The wild dogs were attacking one of the herd.

I continued struggling and sweating, trying to wriggle a hand out. We struck match after match but mostly burned ourselves. I felt something give, but we were still bound tight. Finally, just as I was beginning to think we'd never get free, the ropes loosened. Several threads fell away. I pulled hard, desperate now. James cried out. My hand broke free. I untied my other wrist and then James'. I stood, rubbing my sore, singed forearm, checking how bad the burns were.

I looked up and towards the undergrowth. We were being watched again. One of the wild dogs was back. Its muzzle was smeared with fresh blood. It licked its lips.

"Get up James!" Another wild dog appeared—and another. "They're back."

"What?!"

"Look dominant. Bare your teeth," I said, trying myself to stand tall and look masterful.

James said, "*They* aren't going to be impressed with *our* teeth, are they?"

Something different moved behind us. I looked for a tree to climb. None had low branches. Or lianas. There was no safe place.

I didn't dare breathe. The new sound wasn't a wild dog. It was much larger. The dogs turned. The noise of the approaching animal grew louder. Much louder. One of the dogs ran away whining, its tail between its legs. If the wild dogs were frightened, this—whateveritwas—had to be very bad news.

Agamid or 'blood-sucker' –
"a chisel-toothed lizard, with a bright orange head
and shoulders and was doing push-ups"

2
PHONE CALL

Before I continue with my story and you find out what frightened the wild dogs away, I should explain how we ended up alone in the jungle. I need to start my story from the beginning: the day I took a phone call that changed everything.

The scent of incense floated in through the window on a normal day at home. Someone rang the bell at the little shrine to Ganesh* just across the street from our house.

The land line rang. It was all crackle and hiss. It had to be our parents.

"*Kahan porio**?" A deep male voice asked. That was odd. Usually the phone operators were women.

"This is Alexander in Kathmandu. Who's calling?"

There was a terrific clunk that made my ears ring. There

15

were more crackles, then Dad's voice. "Hi—how's things?"

"Okay."

"Ready for your trip?"

"Yeah, definitely." I was really looking forward to getting back to the forest. Back to our parents to help with their work on rare wildlife. And to chill—away from teachers and traffic and timetables and stuff.

"Umm. I have a chore for you."

"That's unusual."

"Sorry, Ali, but you know how difficult it is for us to get things down here."

"Yeah, yeah. So what have I got to do now?"

"I need you to go over to Brian's office and pick up a small parcel. This afternoon. Is that okay?"

"Yeah, yeah." I wished he wouldn't do that. He knew I couldn't exactly say no. "What's so important?"

"Oh. Err. Umm. Just don't forget, will you? It's...err... really important. Yes...umm...crucial. Umm...so...how's school?"

"It's okay—look Dad, you don't have to make polite conversation. And I won't forget. I'm not totally useless, you know."

"Yes, okay. So you remember where to get off the bus? They...err...we'll...try to send someone to meet you. All right?"

"Yeah, 'course. Is Mum there?"

Mum came on and started to gush. Suddenly, she uttered an odd yelp as if the phone had been snatched away. There were male Nepali voices. Then, the phone went dead. That was odd. The whole phone call had been completely weird.

16

"A friendly little house gecko whispered
shee-sheet-shatshat
from the ceiling above me"

A friendly little house gecko whispered *shee-sheet-shat-shat* from the ceiling above me. He moved forward—stalking a fat mosquito. He lunged at it, and I saw blood in the gecko's mouth as he swallowed it down. The mosquito had probably fed on me last night. The gecko licked its lips, and then it licked its eyes.

James burst in through the door and threw down his bag. He looked—as usual—like he'd been dragged around the playground a few times. His hair was an unnatural sandy colour. Laxmi *tut-tutted* at the state he was in.

"Come see what I have prepared for you, boys."

We could already smell her delicious sizzling fried snacks. Laxmi always cooked the most amazing treats; somehow she turned boring vegetables into the tastiest foods imaginable.

"You've got a new zit, Alex."

"Thanks for noticing."

Laxmi was with us when we stepped out of our house before dawn the next day. It didn't take her long to find a taxi. She woke the driver who was sleeping inside. He stretched, burped, started the engine of his beaten-up old car and did a U-turn without really looking or waking up. We waved goodbye to Laxmi out of the window as the taxi sped away.

Not long after the sun had come up, we climbed the wobbly steps onto a Royal Nepal Airways Twin Otter, bound for Nepalgunj. The 18-seater plane was so old that the seats were like canvas camping chairs, and although the smiling stewardess was smaller than me, she had to stoop to avoid hitting her head on the ceiling. She said, "Ah! Alex and Chimes, my good friends! It is nice to see you again, boys!"

We settled in, and I looked out of the window. There were vultures strolling about on the runway, as usual. One propeller and then the other started to turn. Every school holiday, we travelled this way to join our parents. This was the first time on our own, though. I was a bit nervous, but it was cool to be trusted to travel without an adult.

The little plane was soon buzzing over endless green hills and ridges. I suppose we were blazé about amazing views, but the mountains always made me feel insignificant. Huge up-draughts—invisible forces—tossed the plane like an insect.

To the left was flat greenness. To our right were the mighty Himalayas*, great walls of black rock and snow. The views were familiar but always different.

James said, "Snow always makes me think of ice-cream. Glaciers look like where it's dribbled."

"Yeah, stomach-brain." I looked at my brother. You could tell James had dressed in the dark. His shirt buttons were in the wrong holes.

My mind wandered beyond food. I wondered what was inside Dad's important packet. It was probably some boring report or something, but I'd sneak a look later.

We walked into the terminal building of Nepalgunj airport. "*Phwah*," James said. "They still haven't fixed the bogs in this place!"

Millions of flies came and went through the toilet door. It was like fly rush hour. I tried to ignore the rank smells. Our cheerful deaf and dumb porter-friend greeted us with signs and a lopsided grin that showed big gaps between his teeth. He did a long mime-thing about how happy we must be to be going to meet our parents again. Then he did another about how we weren't any fatter. He thought all foreigners are rich and so should be fat. We smiled and nodded. A pale little house gecko made *tut-tut* noises above us.

We stepped outside into dazzling sunshine and soon climbed into a two-wheeled *tanga** pulled by a piebald pony. She trotted as far as the cross-roads where buses waited and where, as always, it reeked of pee and diesel. This place was loud and stinky, but the chaos of the hot, sticky Plains seemed friendlier, newer and livelier than the cooler chaos of the mediaeval city of Kathmandu we'd just left.

"Back in Nepalgunj, eh, James?"

"Yeah," James nodded. "The samosas are the best here."

Several buses revved and blew their horns to call passengers.

"I reckon we've got time for some food, James."

"Of course we have!"

We gobbled down some greasy bus-station snacks, then before the day had seriously heated up, we squeezed onto a jam-packed bus. While we waited for it to set off, I watched small children playing with bicycle wheel hoops, a car made from a box and a bit of metal pipe, and a food tin pushed along with a stick. Finally, the bus moved off slowly, horn-honking in case any last minute passengers wanted to get on. We were soon rattling and bumping along the pot-holed and rutted main road taking us further west.

3
JUNGLE RENDEZVOUS

I was jolted awake. There was a chipped enamel plate in front of my face. Triangles of coconut rocked on it. A fly rode on one piece as if it was on a tiny rocking horse.

The skinny little girl who held the plate said, "One rupees only!"

James woke too. He rummaged for coins and bought some. The girl disappeared, and then the plate came in through the next glassless window of the beaten up old bus. I stuck my head out. The girl was standing on a tiny ledge that ran along the side of the bus, on just the ends of her two big toes. The driver honked a warning, revved the engine and the girl jumped clear without anything falling off her plate. The bus moved on. The coconut let out a satisfying *snap* as I sank my teeth into it.

By now, it felt like we'd been travelling for days, though we'd only left our house that morning. We had made the short bumpy flight to stinky old Nepalgunj Airport, and now—on the bus—sweat stuck my backside to the seat. I thought about putting my head out of the window again. It might be cooler, but people puke so much on these trips you risk getting a face full. I stared ahead, clutching my backpack. I was dying to see what was in the parcel, but now wasn't the time.

I began checking off landmarks along the East-West Highway: the Shiva* shrine, the broken bridge where the bus had to drive down into the dry river bed, the long sweeping bend, the crossroads with the big billboard advertising the latest Hindi films and a particularly impressive red silk-cotton tree.

We came to a sign—oddly it was in English—saying SLOW—MEN AT WORK.

"I can't believe they *still* haven't finished building this road!" I said as our bus slowed and showered the labourers in even more dust. It stuck to the triangles of sick below some of the windows on the bus. Most of the road-workers were women who had babies tied onto their backs. They had to break up big rocks into smaller pieces to be used for the road base. The babies cried as the women squatted, tap-tapping at the stones.

"Look," James said. "They've all got bleeding hands. They haven't even got band-aids." They'd used manky old scraps of cloth as bandages.

Further on in a dry gully, a troop of langurs sat on their bottoms, arms resting on bent knees; they looked almost human. Even their hands—with thumbs and fingernails—were like ours. They had big, bright, don't-shout-at-me eyes. A halo of white fur stood out all around their black faces as if something had scared them. Other members of the troop were

"Langurs have complex stomachs"

browsing in trees that overhung the riverbed. Their furry tails looked like something you'd pull to make a church bell ring.

James said, "Those monkeys are just like a bunch of hoodies hanging around with nothing to do. Hey, one is scratching its armpit!"

"Langurs, not monkeys, James."

"Pedant."

"Primate."

"Neanderthal."

"Hey, I've read that langurs have complex stomachs,

23

which allow them to ferment their food to get all the goodness out of it."

"I've got a complex stomach," James said patting his. He let a fart go and announced, "I ferment things too."

"Oh do shut up, James..."

He only stopped talking for a couple of seconds, then, "What are we going to do when we get off the bus?"

"Dunno."

"Do you think Mum or Dad will meet us, Alex?"

"Err, Dad said something about sending someone to meet us, but he seemed even vaguer than usual."

"So—they'll be in camp?"

"Of course they will."

"What if they're not?" James said.

"Why wouldn't they be?" I just couldn't explain why I had a bad feeling ever since that phone call.

We both went back to staring out of the window. There were still miles to go in this clapped out old bus. It crawled along, farting black stuff out of its back end and rattling so much it sounded like bits should be falling off along the road.

The day was cooling a bit by the time the bus shuddered to a halt. I nudged James. "Wake up. We're nearly there."

James grunted and sat up. A bored-looking soldier with an ancient rifle raised the barrier to allow the bus to drive into the Royal Bardiya National Park.

Guns. There were too many weapons in this country. My guts contracted in nervousness, but there was no reason to feel like that. I was hyper-alert now. I needed to focus on the scenery—looking out for familiar landmarks.

After a few more miles, I staggered forward and asked the

driver to let us down. As the bus slowed, though, I wondered if this really was the right place. We stumbled off anyway, glad to escape the stink inside. I watched as the bus, still belching its nasty black mechanical diarrhoea, shrank to a small smut on the horizon. I didn't want to be left behind. I clutched my backpack.

James grabbed my sleeve. "You sure this is the right place?"

"Err...yeah. Been here loads of times. Don't you recognise it?"

"No."

A couple of narrow, well-used paths led into the jungle, but one patch of sal* forest looks very like any other. The trees here—just like in much of Nepal's lowlands—were tall, straight and smooth-barked. Impossible to climb. It was weird to think that sal wood is so heavy, it sinks in water. I peered up to the dusty tree-tops, tracing lianas dangling from high branches and strangler figs that squeeze the life out of trees, slowly replacing them with greedy green latticework. I really wasn't sure we were in the right place.

A twig snapped. We turned. A small thin boy had magically appeared. He must have been squatting in the shade of the roadside undergrowth watching us.

"You are Flaming?" he asked.

"Flaming? Flaming what?"

"You are the Flaming boys, yes?"

"Ah, yeah, I'm Alex Fleming."

"You are animal boys, yes?"

"What?"

"Your father and mother, they like the animals?

"Yeah."

"Come!" He turned back into the forest, beckoning us the way Nepalis do, palm downwards, like they are wafting a fart. His shorts had patches upon patches.

The boy walked off the tarmacked road and into the jungle. James shouldered his pack. "Where's he taking us, Alex?"

"Seems like the right direction for camp."

James whispered, "How do we know we can trust him?"

"We don't...but Dad said they'd send someone, so it should be okay." *They?* Why had Dad said "they"?

The boy turned round, like he was checking on us. We pretended we weren't talking. He picked his nose while he waited for us to catch up.

There was a noise of something moving behind me. I spun around. A raucous, mocking laugh. Why was I so nervous? It was only a woodpecker, scampering up the tree trunk closest to me. A shaft of sunlight caught his wing feathers so they gleamed golden. He cackled again.

This was the jungle Kipling wrote about in The Jungle Book—dry forest of tall naked trees and dusty termite mounds. I thought I'd feel good to be back. After so long in the city, the dust and mouldering leaves smelt familiar, but even the loud squawk of a parakeet scared me. I couldn't work out why I was so on edge.

"Look—rhino poop," James said. He'd noticed a scattering of tennis-ball sized dollops of dried dung. "We'd better keep a look out for poachers' traps."

"Don't you mean hefferlump traps?"

"A great Indian rhinoceros lifted its nose to sniff the air"

"No. Don't speak to me like that. I've been out tracking with Ramdin. He's told me so much interesting stuff. He says rhinos back into their loo spots. They keep coming back to the same places but don't look behind them, so that's where the poachers dig the trap: the rhino walks backward to poop and then falls into the hole!"

"Rhinos aren't too bright, then!" I gave him a brotherly slap his between the shoulder-blades. "We'd better make plenty of noise so they hear us coming and don't charge at us by mistake." Then I said, "But since when did rhinos have the manners to 'go to the loo'? You'll be saying they use bog-paper next!"

"Shut up. You're always interrupting and you're always treating me like a baby. You never listen and never believe anything I tell you either..."

James stomped on ahead in a sulk, but he couldn't keep quiet for long. "You know it would be really easy..." James stopped speaking as he saw that the boy was listening. We walked on, in silence for a while. Then James whispered, "It would be really easy... to lose a couple of bodies in the jungle. Leopards and vultures would eat the evidence."

"Enough, James...."

The boy looked around, beckoned again and said, "Come!"

"Okay, okay, we're coming."

Then, "Hey, you feel something, James?"

"Yeah, yeah I feel it," he said, whispering still. "What is it?"

"I remember getting a kind of creepy feeling in the back of my neck last time we were in amongst that big herd of she-elephants and calves."

We looked at each other. "Elephants!"

"Hey, I noticed some ele-poop back there too. It was still steaming."

There was the softest sound, like someone close-by walking in over-large bedroom slippers. Then there was a deep resonating fart. Bushes parted just up ahead. The long grey face of a huge tuskless cow elephant appeared. Her ears flapped and she raised her wrinkled trunk to get a better smell of us. There was movement on either side of the first elephant and two more faces appeared. An amazingly deep rumbling noise came from the one on the left. The other two elephants replied.

I nudged James. "Sneak away."

"Don't be stupid!"

The rumbling became louder as the three of them discussed the three of us. Gradually, other elephants joined them. The three leaders moved closer and started flapping their ears and blowing down their trunks. I wasn't too worried. This was just a display and I didn't think that elephants usually chased people. The middle one let out an ear-splitting trumpet.

There was a noise behind me. I turned to see the ragged boy running. He was disappearing fast between the trees. It took me a few second to realise why. He'd heard the matriarch* break into a charge. Elephants don't look as if they can sprint, but they can move surprisingly fast. Now I could feel the ground vibrating as the biggest, oldest cow elephant in the herd came pounding towards us. I pelted off after the boy. James was on my heels.

We ran like panicking deer. We ran till the sweat streamed off us. We ran till we were fit to burst. The clumsy sounds of my own feet and the noise of my backpack slapping against my back made it hard to be sure whether she was still chasing us, but at least I could hear gasping sounds from James, so I knew he was behind me.

Finally we slowed to a stop, hands on hips, panting, "Can't... go... on."

The matriarch was nowhere to be seen. I had a big stitch in my side. Once I'd got my breath back, I realised I had no idea where the path was, nor which direction our parents camp was in. I rummaged for my compass.

"Have we lost the boy now?" James gasped.

We hadn't. There was a whistle. We saw him through the trees, beckoning us again.

"*Badmass* haati*," he mumbled as we caught him up.

"Yeah, very *badmass*," James agreed.

We followed the boy for a long time, then we joined a path I recognised. "*Pssst*. Slow up."

James gave me a puzzled look.

"I reckon I can find the way to our camp from here."

29

I gestured towards the boy. "He could be with a gang or something. They might rob us."

"Have we got anything worth stealing?"

"Not sure. Let's hang back." The boy strode further and further ahead. "Quick, James. You go that way, I'll go this and we'll meet around the back of that big red silk cotton tree in a few minutes. If he turns round, just lie down and keep still." We sprinted off in different directions. I was impressed at how quickly I lost sight of James. I prayed he wouldn't get himself lost. I lay flat in amongst some prickly dry leaves and watched the boy slowly double back, searching. He seemed bored. He looked towards me and for a moment I was sure he'd seen me. I let my head sink right down and held my breath. I listened for sounds of him moving, then when I heard nothing for a while gingerly raised my head. The boy had wandered away. When I was sure he'd given up looking for us, I circled around to the big red silk cotton tree.

James was there waiting, grinning. "It worked! We've lost him."

"Yeah. So let's have drink and go on towards camp." We were so looking forward to seeing Mum and Dad and finding out what they'd been doing.

At first we ran, but that wasn't easy with all the overhanging branches, and the heat was sapping. We slowed to a walk. We trudged through the crunchy leaf-litter. Overhead, troops of unfriendly rhesus monkeys chattered at us, mocking us.

"Hey! I'm hungry," James announced.

"You're always hungry!" I said.

Then, "No actually I'm not hungry, I'm STARVING."

We stopped. I squatted down. I tipped out the contents of our backpacks. I pulled out an untidy parcel containing some food. We found a log and sat down. We squidged bananas between deformed hunks of bread. James mumbled through a full mouth, "Wish you could learn to cut straight slices."

"It all tastes the same. Stop complaining."

All of a sudden there was a scampering sound. A small furry hand grabbed my food. The hand had fingernails just like mine, and they were just as dirty.

"Oi!" I shouted. "Come back!" I shouted as I chased after him. The monkey-thief was fast. He didn't even look back as he shot back up the tree to enjoy my lunch. James shrieked as another rhesus monkey reached into my backpack. "Alex! Look!"

The second monkey cantered away awkwardly with a bigger prize. I realised that the big brown envelope—Dad's important envelope—was clutched to its chest.

"The Rhesus Macaque ran off with Dad's important envelope."

4
THIEF!

"What was in that envelope?" James asked.

"'Dunno."

"Was it important?"

"Probably. Dad's tone of voice said it was."

Up in the high branches, the monkey bared his teeth at us. "Look. It's ripping into the envelope. It thinks it's food!"

The monkey pulled out a thick wad of elephant-grey banknotes.

"Money!" I stuttered.

The monkey sniffed his prize. A single thousand-rupee note floated down.

"Hey, I can see big bundles of cash!" James said. "That's a lot of money."

"Yeah." I ran over to pick up the thousand rupees.

Now the monkey knew there was no food in the packet, it lost interest and stuffed it in a crook of his unclimbable tree. Another note sailed silently down. The monkey showed his disgust by weeing on us.

"*Aggh*!" James spat and wiped his mouth with his sleeve.

I stood looking up and tasted wee too, but my head was busy with more important things. "What's going on, James? If that envelope is full of rupees, I reckon there could be five million in that packet. That's what, five thousand pounds?! What was Dad thinking, to trust us with five thousand quid? And why wouldn't they tell us we were carrying so much money?"

"Yeah. Weird. We've got to get it back, Alex."

"Let's show the monkey our food."

Waving sandwiches only made the monkey bare its teeth again.

"It doesn't like you, Alex."

"Let's throw things at it, then maybe the monkey will throw things back."

But there were no stones in this sandy place.

James wandered away. I cursed him. He's always going off when there are things to do.

A little later, he came back carrying an armful of bits he'd broken off a termites' nest. Dropping his ammo at his feet, he announced, "We can throw these!"

We're both good at cricket and started firing termite house at the thief. When one of my missiles hit the monkey on the nose, James shouted a celebratory, *"Howsatt*!"

It didn't make the monkey drop the packet. It just weed on us some more and chattered its disgust. It scooped up the envelope again, scampered higher, ripped some more pieces off it and—ever hopeful—nibbled a banknote. Two more grey-blue thousand-rupee notes drifted down. James ran to catch them, but I wondered what the point was. Two thousand rupees was nothing. Then something else moved up in the tree tops. A second monkey approached our thief. I held my breath. The intruder was bigger. The dominant male probably.

There was a fight and a lot of shrieks. Bits of stick fell. More wee. Then the big brown envelope hit the ground with a thud. Separate brand-new banknotes rained down like a slow motion, giant grey snowstorm. James ran about like a mad thing catching them and gathering up handfuls. I sat mesmerised by the way the money floated down around us. I was so relieved I did nothing for a while. There was a soft sad *oo-oooing* of an emerald dove.

Finally, I had to rouse myself. I walked over to the envelope. The 1000-rupee notes in the packet were bound up in wads of hundred. The rest had scattered over a surprisingly large area, but I suddenly felt really tired and couldn't be bothered to help James. "We must have got nearly all the money," I muttered.

"Yeah, it looks about right. I thought we'd lost it for good!"

"Yeah. Me too."

Birds were growing noisy as the heat of the day was fading. The late afternoon air became thick and heavy with scent from the slim naked sal trees. "We'd better get going. It's still a long way to our camp."

James nodded. We swallowed down some water and set off. It felt good to have the full pack on my back. In this part of the forest the trees shaded out lots of light so there wasn't much growing at ground level. The walking was easy enough. James whistled tunelessly to himself. The leaf litter grew deeper. Some leaves were the size of tennis racquets. Apparently, James no longer felt tired because he kicked through them, sending brown showers up into the air.

"Oi! What's wrong with you? Be quiet!"

There was an alarm-bark from a spotted deer. "*Shh*. Stop for a minute. Listen." A faint breeze moved the small leaves in the bushes that surrounded us. I was imagining dangers. I told myself to calm down. "Oh look, try these." I picked some curry leaves and gave James a handful.

He stuffed some into his mouth, and said a muffled, "Mmm, not bad." He picked more. "Pity they're not very filling."

We trudged on in silence, one behind the other, for a long while.

Maybe an hour later, James stopped and turned around to me. "What's that smell?"

He followed his nose to a messy patch of leaf litter. There were smears of fresh blood.

"A tiger kill! Look, there's a little deer hoof. Maybe we could barbecue what's left! Look, I've got matches..."

"We've got to get away from here!" I said.

"Yeah, all right, but there are some nice-looking curry leaves—look."

There was a terrific shriek from above us. A troop of lanky langurs let out a volley of alarm barks, *kak kak kak kak*. It rained monkey wee again.

"We really, *really* need to get away from here James!" I grabbed his clothes and tried to pull him away from the curry bush. "Come on!" He was intent on grabbing more to stuff into his mouth, but an odd double snort made him look up from his leaf plucking. Everything was the same colour, but I saw something amongst the trees. Then what I thought was a big boulder moved. A great Indian rhinoceros lifted its nose and huge single horn to sniff the air. It seemed to be peering short-sightedly at us. Supposedly rhinos can't see that well and mostly make sense of their world through hearing and smell. I put a finger into my mouth to wet it. I held it up. The rhino was downwind. It could smell us.

It snorted crossly again.

My mind went into overdrive. Rhinos aren't too bright. You can never tell what they might do. If a rhino gets spooked, it'll charge blindly and often in the wrong direction. That's what Ramdin, our parents' research assistant, had told us.

There was a shuffling sound behind me. I turned and saw a smaller grey shape. The rhino had a calf and we were standing between it and its mother. The stupid calf took a few steps towards us. A bad move.

I whispered to James, "If she charges, get behind a tree— or up one—or lie down quietly."

"What?" James replied. He was concentrating so much on selecting the youngest, tastiest curry leaves he hadn't registered we had company. Now though he whipped round then slowly squatted down without saying another word. In my head, I was still trying to convince myself we weren't in danger, but our voices spooked the rhino. She snorted again, and broke into a charge—straight towards us. Ramdin was wrong about them usually charging in the wrong direction.

James must have had rockets up his bottom for he shot up an impossible-to-climb tree. I looked around, wildly. There were no trees I could get up. I started to run.

Domph, domph domph: the dreadful sound of one-and-a-half-tonnes of charging rhino came after me. Rhinos might look as if they are wearing heavy, bolt-on armour, but this one was fast.

Desperately, I looked for refuge as I sprinted between the trees. She was gaining on me. I dodged, but she still followed. She was nimble. She was getting closer. So close. I turned. She turned. I'm quite a good runner. Why couldn't I out-dodge this great lumbering beast? Then just when I felt she must be near enough to trample me, I dived off to the side and went skidding on my belly in the leaf litter.

She turned in a surprisingly short distance. She charged again. This time I stayed low. I monkey-crawled to the nearest big tree and tried to hide my outline behind it. She pounded past me. Then she stopped. She lifted up her nose, trying to sniff me out. I held my breath. There was a grunt from the calf and the mother rhino turned towards her baby.

In that split second, I sprinted for a tree with a few low branches. I discovered tree-climbing skills I didn't know I had. I found myself standing, shaky-legged, on a branch three metres above the forest floor. Then I watched the mother swerve around to rejoin her baby and they trotted away like ponies. I gazed after her vast receding bullet-proof backside.

I slid down to ground level.

"James! JAMES, WHERE ARE YOU?" I ran back the way I thought I'd come. Nothing. I ran back further. I shouted.

Nothing but the small sounds of settling leaf litter. My heart was thumping. I shouted again. My voice cracked. A cicada started up. A mosquito buzzed around my sweaty face.

This was serious. I had no idea which way the path was. I was lost. Alone. And darkness was gathering fast.

5
ALONE

I was fighting back tears. I shouted again. Still nothing.

No one's allowed to stay in the National Park after dark, unless they have a special permit. The authorities knew about my parents, of course, and the soldiers who guarded the wildlife dropped by from time to time for a mug of tea. Sometimes they'd even come out with us on survey trips, but they had guns. And Dad said that the soldiers tended to shoot first and ask questions afterwards. With Maoists about, the soldiers got a bit jumpy. We never felt safe around them.

If I lit a fire, would they come and arrest me? Surely they wouldn't shoot without saying something? I really wasn't sure. I did know that Dad said the soldiers often sleep on duty. Surely then it was better to risk them than being eaten by some hungry animal?

What was James doing? He might be okay. He never seemed scared of anything. No imagination. Not like me. I scrunched up my eyes. I wasn't going to cry. I had to man up.

I needed to light a fire. I just had to hope James would smell it or see it and find me. I collected sticks, some the size of matches and others that were bigger. I tried to arrange the smallest in a criss-cross pile, but my hands were shaking so much it took several attempts. You have to be patient to light a one-match fire. Finally, the small kindling was arranged properly. I struck a match and the sticks caught fire nicely. It flared as I carefully placed bigger pieces on top. It started to crackle, and I felt a little more under control. If the park guards saw it, they'd help surely. It was a comfort and the fire would keep big cats away— and mosquitoes.

I so wished James was with me.

There was a spine-chilling *awooom* from a tigress. Close. Probably she was watching—me or James. I took a gulp of warm, plastic-flavoured water. It was my last drink. I'd drained my bottle.

I shivered, though I wasn't cold. Not at all. I didn't want to spend a night alone. I noticed an ace-of-clubs footprint in the dusty ground. Rhino.

"Bloody rhino! It's your fault—all of this!"

I went through the routine of clearing a patch of leaf litter so I could lie down—and not get bitten by ants. I don't know why I bothered though, because I couldn't rest. I lay flat on my back. My guts rumbled. It felt as if my stomach was touching my spine, I was that hungry. I looked up at the black leaf-shapes that blotted out most of the stars. I sat up. I took off my shoes to try and make myself more comfortable, more like I was going to bed, but then I just sat there. It was going to be a long, long night. My mind got stuck at the thought that predators hunt at night. When I'd slept out in the forest before—with my parents—the sounds were interesting and soothing. Now that I was here alone, they announced a plethora of things that might bite, sting, or eat me.

What was James doing? Was he sleeping or searching for me? I strained my ears, listening for his shouts. Nothing. I lay down. The ground was brick-hard. I rolled over and tried to make a pillow with my arm.

I must have slept—finally, for a while—because I woke to an awful sound, part cry, part blood-curdling shriek. In my sleepy fog, I was sure it must be a ghost. Then as I calmed down, I realised it was probably an owl.

I remembered that our parents had chosen to work in this part of the huge forest reserve because it was close to where Mum first saw bear tracks. Bears. Sloth bears. They can be really aggressive. The fire was only a few glowing red embers now. I threw on more wood to act as a bear-repellent. I needed to focus on something else, anything else! Think about skipping school. About missing Miss Hepplethwaithe's sarcasm. About avoiding homework. About not being back for the exams.

I couldn't forget where I was though. There were so many spooky sounds that I couldn't identify. And something was moving on the forest floor close by.

It wasn't a large animal, but it rustled the leaf litter. It didn't sound like a snake. Or did it? It was coming closer. No, not *it*—there were two of them. They sounded as large as rats—or maybe bigger. I rolled over towards my backpack and slowly, quietly rummaged for my flashlight. Why hadn't I got it out before? I rolled back towards the sound, switched on, and saw—nothing.

I scanned around with the light. Was I imagining things? What if I was losing it?

Then some dry leaves moved by themselves.

I didn't really want to but I got up and crept over to see. It was a scorpion. How could such a small creature sound so large? I looked closer and realised it was actually a pair of scorpions. The male had a hold of the female's pincers and was trying to pull her about like a ballroom dancer. They were doing a wedding dance. It was quite sweet, but I knew I'd be in trouble if I rolled on one. Mum said it hurts for days if you get stung.

I returned to my lonely patch of forest floor, stretched out and lay there thinking how good it would be to be able to drop off to sleep—and stay asleep. I couldn't stop thinking about scorpion stings and snake bites. Scorpion stings. Snake Bites. Snakes, scorpions, spiders, ticks, leeches, blister beetles, centipedes. Which was worst? How much would they hurt?

I threw another bit of wood on the fire and switched off my light. I needed to save the battery. I tuned into new sounds. There were rustlings close by. And snuffling noises. What now? I turned my flashlight on again and looked around. Again, I saw nothing at first. Then, in the trembling spotlight, I made out a round creature. It was as startled and confused as I was. For a few seconds it was frozen to the spot. It didn't even twitch a whisker. It stared with big cute eyes. Then, as I started to laugh, it returned to its work, sniffing around amongst the dry leaves as if I wasn't there. It wasn't frightened of me at all. Those long, long quills must defend it quite well. Dinesh says porcupine tastes good, but I wonder how people catch them and avoid the quills. He told us a story of a leopard that tried to eat a porcupine and got quills stuck into its front paw. The foot got terribly infected and the leopard died slowly.

I lay back. I couldn't get comfortable. Couldn't stop thinking about James, and guns and death and disease. I had to find James. I wanted to pray that a man-eater wouldn't take James—or me, but I didn't know which was the right god to ask.

I must have drifted off into another cat-nap. A loud *CRACK* woke me with a start. Something big had trodden on a twig. I think I'd cried out. I was wide awake now. What had dragged me into consciousness? I lay. I listened. I didn't dare breathe. There were more sounds. It was heading towards me. Straight towards me. It wasn't a deer or anything delicate. It was at least the size of a leopard. Leopards are the most dangerous predators in the jungle. They're cunning and some have a taste for human meat. I couldn't protect myself. The tall, smooth-trunked sal trees around me had no side-branches. I couldn't even climb to safety. I didn't even have a stick to stir up the fire.

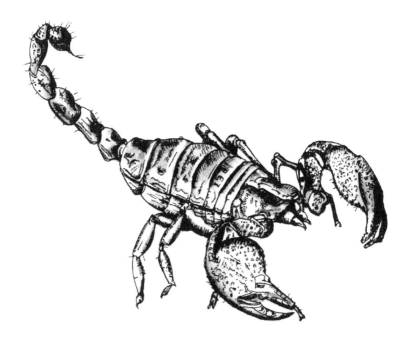

"Scorpion stings hurt for days"

6
LOST AND FOUND

I sat up, holding my breath. My mouth felt as dry as a desert. I couldn't stop myself from shaking.

Breaking the silence was an odd reverberating sort of noise. I grabbed the flashlight. I switched it on and pointed towards the sound. I scanned around. My brother appeared, standing in the spotlight. His hand went up to his face to shield his eyes from the glare of the light, but I could see he was grinning. He let out another thunderous fart as he strode towards me. I was so relieved, so pleased to see him, I wasn't even rude—which was a first. In fact, I was all choked up.

I kicked the fire and sparks flew up making it easier to see. He came closer. He must have been really pleased to see me too, because he held out his arms as if he wanted to give me a big man-hug. He's never wanted to hug me before. I've never wanted to hug him either, but as I scrambled to my feet, the stench hit me. "*Pwhah*! What's that stink? Is it you?"

He pulled away, wiping snot and tears from his face. "Umm. I had an accident..."

"*Aghh*, you didn't!" I said putting my hand over my face.

"No, not *that* kind of accident. I fell into a pit in the dark back there. It was deep and soft and warm. The soft stuff was rhino dung. Must have been a poachers' trap."

"A trap? Really?"

"Yeah." He stood there hands on hips, hair standing on end and poop all over his face and probably everywhere else.

"Okay. Sorry. Go on then. I'm listening. Look, it's really good to see you, but take two steps back, will you?"

Standing his ground, he continued, "So anyway—as I was saying—this hole was really manky, and it was difficult to climb out. I fell back in several times so I got really plastered in the stuff. No water to wash, of course." He wiped his still-snotty nose with the back of his hand again and made a nasty streak across his face.

"S'pose I should say it's good to see you."

"Whatever. Lighting the fire was a brilliant idea, Alex... that's how I found you," he said. "I smelled the burning wood."

"I'm surprised you could smell anything!"

"Huh. Anything to eat?" He asked.

"No. Hungry?"

"Starving." We sat in silence for a while.

"Look, we should find more wood and stoke up the fire. And maybe if we think of horrible food, we won't feel so bad."

"Bounty bars—they're worst," James said. "They smell like suntan lotion."

That made me imagine cream—being poured over a huge hunk of chocolate cake. "Bounty isn't that bad. I'd kill for one now."

"Yeah, me too."

"This isn't working, James! How about school broccoli floating in green water?"

"Yeah! Or jellied eels."

"Yeah, wobbly and black and slimy." James said. "Imagine being served up jellied eels and lumpy school custard."

Imagining that made me feel sick, but it didn't take away the hunger pangs. Several minutes had gone by when I hadn't worried about my parents. That set me worrying again.

James prattled on, "I'd get a tiny spoon and eat the bit of custard that wasn't next to the fish...."

"Hmm... you always did have weird tastes, James. Look, can you think or something else to talk about?"

"Nah."

"Let's get some sleep then. We'll find our way to the camp early tomorrow. Better start at dawn."

He looked sulky, but didn't say any more. We settled down, relieved to be together again—despite James' rhino dung perfume, and our gnawing hunger, and James' childishness.

Next morning, the first thing I thought about was food. We were cold, damp and still starving. I rooted out the compass from my backpack.

"Let's get going." Then, "*Phwah!* You still stink—enough to make a lady rhino follow you."

"Get lost."

"Look, the camp's only about five more miles..." I was guessing, but trying to sound confident. "Let's get there."

As we were packing James said, "Look—porky-pine footprints. One must have come close last night. I wish I'd seen it."

"I did see it. And they're called *porcupines*."

"I know, but porky-pines sounds nicer, and it reminds me of pork pies. Arjun says they taste almost as nice too—like chicken," James said, licking his lips.

"Neanderthal!"

"You need some new insults, Alex."

"Do you reckon that Arjun has eaten all the things he says he has?"

"Yeah, why wouldn't he? It might not be legal, but he is a policeman!"

"It's just that he describes everything as tasting like chicken—even snake."

"Hmm, snake. I'm hungry enough to try some..." he grinned. "Okay then, let's catch the next snake we see and barbeque it."

"No time, James."

Walking on, spiky shrubs and creepers caught our clothes. One particularly vicious-looking bush barred my way. Insects were impaled on several thorns. Some bugs were still alive and waved their legs in a pathetic attempt to get free. A small bird was watching; it had a dark eye-stripe so looked like it was frowning. It made a sound like a telephone ringing: the butcher-bird was telling us to stay clear of his revolting breakfast.

"When will we find something to eat?" James whined.

"You could help yourself to some bird-food!" Then, "Look. We need to keep going."

We hurried on at a brisk trot, while the heat of the day built up quickly. We scared a huge herd of spotted deer. The stag turned, showing off his fine lyre-shaped antlers. He barked in alarm and his herd bounded gracefully away. Two very sick-looking animals at the back had trouble keeping up with the others; their fur looked moth-eaten.

"Dad says they should shoot some spotted deer, then the meat could feed the people that go hungry outside the Park."

"Sounds like a good idea," James said, but I could tell he was thinking about Dad, not the deer.

"Except it is against the law in Nepal, and sentimental people in Western countries don't think you should shoot wild animals. People who say that can never have gone hungry," I said rubbing my empty belly.

"Mmm," James said in a way that meant he wasn't listening. And anyway, I was too breathless now for speeches...

This dry sal forest was a weird environment. Nepalis call it jungle, but that's the word they use for uncultivated land. Most of the time you feel as if you can see a long way ahead, but it's oh so easy to walk round in circles. You often get taken by surprise too—by almost walking into things like a stray elephant or a sun-bathing python. My head was somewhere in Kipling's story of the Elephant's Child when a red-brown blur shot off like a bullet from just under my feet. I cried out in shock. Why it spooked me, I don't know. It was only a week-old spotted deer. I'd almost stepped on it.

I decided the best way to keep walking in a straight line was to look ahead to a termite mound, and walk to towards it, then repeat the process. Up ahead, I could see the forest had been disturbed. I really hoped that this was Mum and Dad's camp, but it turned out to be a place visited by disgruntled elephants. Trees had been snapped or simply pushed over as if the elephant had had a temper tantrum. Maybe it had. They are increasingly forced into smaller and smaller areas, yet they really really need space.

On we walked, feeling hotter and hotter by the minute. Birds in the trees above us gasped open-beaked. Had we walked past our parents' camp? That would be easy in this jungle. We came to a place where someone had camped. There was burned wood, but no one had been there for months. Had we walked in circles? My hands were shaking as I rummaged for my compass. "Come on, James. This is definitely the right direction." Then, "Yeah, I'm sure this is right."

"You don't *sound* sure, Alex."

A while later, there was a strange sound from somewhere in the treetops. It was like a sail flapping. Above, five flying foxes headed off to raid some mango trees. Their enormous size and weird way of flying made me think of pterodactyls.

Suddenly, I caught a waft of burning wood: a camp fire. A few hundred metres further on, we stumbled up to the edge of our parents' camp.

"Finally," I gasped.

James was about to blunder straight in, but I grabbed his shirt. Everything was so weird about this trip that I wanted to check things out. I put my finger to my mouth in a silent "*Shhh*" and pulled him down so we were squatting in amongst some curry bushes.

We had made the camp quite comfortable by sweeping out the leaves and making a hearth for cooking. We'd even built a table of sorts. Today, though, things weren't right. Someone had trashed the camp and kicked the table to bits, and the place was littered with onion skins, vegetable peelings, and discarded packets. There were so many flies. And a pungent smell of pee. I couldn't see our parents, and this wasn't how Mum and Dad would live. Ramdin and the other field assistants didn't seem to be there either, but a couple of strangers snored by the cooking fire. The only other movement was from two hyperactive scaly pin-striped skinks. There was definitely no sign of our parents. They could be out tracking animals, but that didn't seem likely.

"Where are they?" James asked, his mouth full of curry leaves again.

"Don't know." I whispered. "Let's watch for a bit. With any luck, we'll get some clues about what is going on." I hoped we hadn't lost the advantage of surprise.

It was still very hot. We were parched and desperate for a drink, but we lay in the undergrowth listening. My heart was beating so hard I was sure someone would hear it. There was a muffled squeak from James.

"Shut up!" I hissed.

"Ants are biting my belly." He uttered another suppressed "Ouch!"

"SHUT UP, will you!"

A sound from close behind made me turn with a start. A stranger was standing over us. He wore combats and looked tough. Dark glasses hid his eyes.

"You're late," he said in a remarkably deep voice for such a small man. He pointed a hand-gun at us. "Get up!"

As he marched us into the camp, he kicked the sleeping men awake, swearing at them. He seemed not to care who he pointed the gun at.

I took a deep breath, "Where are our parents?" I tried to sound strong and grown up, but my voice was all high-pitched.

"Where's the money?"

"We want to see our parents."

"So you do have the money with you?" Before I could answer, he wrinkled his nose and said, "*Uuh*, what's that smell?"

"Let us see our parents!" I demanded.

He smiled. The betel* nut he'd been chewing had coloured his teeth red and made him look as if he'd been feeding on someone's blood.

"Go! Sit over there—where I can't smell you, child," he said.

James blurted out, "Can we have a drink—please?" His voiced cracked with the dryness, or maybe he was also fighting back tears.

"Just go! There! Now!"

He ordered us to sit with our backs against a thin sal tree. Roughly he tied my hand left hand to James' right and my right to James' left so we made a circle round the trunk. I stared at him while he was busy, trying to take in the details of his face, so I'd recognise him instantly next time. He was greasy-looking. His face was pock-marked. I wished I could see his eyes.

My phone had fallen out of my pocket and was lying in the dirt beside me. He saw it and, with a hateful look in his eyes, crushed it under his boot. I'd liked my phone, but it would have been no use—with no signal and no charge either.

"Where are our parents?"

He didn't answer.

"Where have you taken them?"

He checked James' bag.

"If you've kidnapped them...you have the money now. You must let them go. Where are they?"

He opened my backpack. He stuffed the money, my solar charger, my compass, and my watch into his pockets and walked off into the forest. The two guards roused themselves reluctantly, scratched, stretched, and followed.

"Oi! Where are you going? You can't...."

He didn't turn. He just kept on walking.

"The heat made this scaly pinstriped skink hyperactive"

*"A hungry pack of Indian Wild Dogs moved in,
looking like they planned to eat us"*

7
LEFT TO BE EATEN ALIVE

That's how we ended up thirsty and trussed up like Christmas turkeys, a succulent dinner for any number of hungry wild animals. That's how we learned that our parents had been kidnapped. We'd kept our side of the bargain. We had brought a ransom and paid the kidnappers, but they hadn't kept their part of the promise. Now we had absolutely no idea where Mum and Dad were or whether they were safe.

We had managed to burn through our ropes, though. We'd used most of a packet of matches. Finally free, I stood, massaging my sore wrists. I was just starting to think about how we'd find our parents, when a hungry pack of Indian Wild Dogs moved in, looking like they planned to eat us. Unbelievably, they didn't.

I smiled when I saw them suddenly take off, with their tails between their legs—until I thought about it. Anything that frightened wild dogs was not going to be good for our health. Their own dinner plans were interrupted when they sensed an even more powerful hunter. We waited, wondering. I reckon I stopped breathing as the noise of a really large animal got closer and closer.

A huge bear covered in shaggy black fur burst out of the undergrowth. She walked pigeon-toed, showing off her curved, slashing claws. She was really close.

Sitting up on her mother's bottom, like a jockey, was a bear cub. We were in serious trouble.

Bears look fluffy, cuddly almost, especially the young ones, but cute they are not. They are solid and powerful, and everyone knows that animals with young are far more unpredictable and aggressive. Things had gone from bad to worse.

I was frozen in indecision. Should we run or keep still?

I needed to think. These sloth bears are short-sighted. Did this one know we were here? I put my finger into my mouth to wet it and check the direction of the breeze. It was coming from her direction towards James and me. She was upwind and couldn't smell us, but she was clearly able to sniff out the wild dogs. She stopped and raised herself up on her hind legs to her full terrifying two-metre height. This unsettled the cub. The mother bear looked around as her cub slipped to the ground. Then, turning back towards the wild dogs, she moved her long fleshy lips as if she was tasting the air as well as sniffing it. The rest of the wild dogs fled; she dropped back onto all fours. The club climbed aboard and she shuffled slowly after them.

It felt like ages had gone by before we dared breathe again. We stood in silence hardly believing our luck.

After a while, I said, "This is crazy. Have you thought about all the endless hours we've spent trying to get even a glimpse of these rare animals? Now we're on the menu—we can't get away from them."

"Nah, we weren't on the menu. Bears only eat roots, fruits, honey and termites, don't they?"

"Maybe, but weren't you around when Arjun said how dangerous the sloth bear is?"

"No, why?"

"They are strong, fearless and not very bright... Arjun says quite a lot of Nepalis get badly slashed by those claws. His grandfather had most of his face taken off by one—and took several weeks to die."

"Wish you hadn't told me that," James said. Then, "I want a drink."

We should have been in a hurry to leave, but we were so thirsty we ransacked the abandoned camp. We didn't even care if the kidnappers came back. First we gulped down a bellyful of water each, then we found some cold rice and vegetable curry and gobbled that down too. Then finally we could sit and think.

"Least they didn't take my wallet." I said patting my back pocket.

"Yeah." James was unusually quiet.

The kidnappers had left us to starve—or be eaten. These were ruthless men, but we *had* to assume they had our parents.

"We've got to follow them, you know."

"Yeah."

What else could we do? They'd taken the ransom money, and—a cold realisation—the kidnappers had no need to keep our Mum and Dad alive. In fact, it would be a lot less hassle if they were dead. Then they couldn't identify their captors. We had to save Mum and Dad.

I leapt up and raced around looking for stuff to put in our backpacks. Fumbling in baskets and boxes, I found rice, matches, and useful bits and pieces. My hands were shaking so much, water splashed everywhere as I refilled our bottles. "C'mon James. This way now. This is the path Deep Voice and his henchmen took and there's not much daylight left."

We needed to move quickly. We needed to catch up.

Dead leaves covered the forest floor, crunching underfoot as we walked. Termites nests as big as us were dotted around like soldiers guarding the forest. One nest had been torn apart recently. The pale termite workers were busily repairing their fortress-home. They waved their jaws, trying to intimidate us. James said, "It smells of bear!"

A bit further on, I heard a sound I didn't want to hear. Someone was stooping over another termite's nest. Surely we hadn't caught up with the kidnappers already? We walked gingerly forward, investigating, trying to keep trees between him and us, so that if he turned and looked in our direction our outlines wouldn't be so obvious. The trouble was that the Sal trees were so thin they were not great for hiding behind. There wasn't much undergrowth either. Ever so slowly we approached. As we got closer I could see that although he was standing up on two legs like a man, he had a long shaggy coat. He was ripping into the colony with his powerful big claws, then blowing away all the dust and stuff. He had rolled his long, dangly top lip up against his nostrils so the dust didn't make him sneeze. When it was all clear, he hoovered up the termites.

We took a detour to avoid disturbing the bear and walked on in silence for ages. Cicadas called, sounding like chain saws. Our progress became slower and slower as we got more and more tired. We really wanted to stop for the night. "Can't we sleep here?" James pleaded.

"Bit further, James. We've got to make use of every minute of daylight."

Soon, the light had failed. It was time to make camp.

"Okay, James. Let's stop here. I'll clear away the leaves. You find some firewood so we can cook rice."

Just the thought of food cheered us and by the time the fire was crackling, our feet weren't throbbing any more. Birds were squawking as the sun began to set. There was a sound just like a goldsmith tap-tapping metal (a coppersmith barbet, I supposed) and there was a pop-popping call of another bird I didn't recognise.

We gobbled down our food, and then James settled down to sleep. He's always been able to sleep anywhere. I wondered how he could, knowing our parents were still in danger. We were in danger, too. Night time is when hunters hunt. I would have to keep watch, but I was so exhausted I wondered how I'd be able to keep myself awake. I needed something to concentrate on. I lay back and tried to trace the courses of lianas that dangled from the tree tops. I studied the outlines of a million kinds of leaves above me. Some were small, some huge, some round, some long, and each moved silently against the twinkling stars beyond. I fell asleep, lulled by the weird jungle noises. I drifted away, dreaming of picnics with my parents. Then I was on a soft bed floating on a sweet rippling ocean of *Coca-Cola* nibbling chocolate biscuits ....

*"The sloth bear was ripping into the termite colony
with his powerful claws"*

8
SWIMMING

I woke, suddenly. It was dawn. Someone was shouting a warning. Deep Voice was standing over me again.

Then the sleep-fog cleared. There was no kidnapper. The sounds came from the squawking and shrieking of a hundred birds. I looked around half expecting my parents to have miraculously arrived while I slept. They hadn't. I was shivering. There was a stone-cold place at the very centre of my stomach. James was breathing deep and slow. I wished I was still asleep too, but the chill made me get up. I was bruised from lying on the rock-hard forest floor. I had a dent in my bum from lying on my wallet. I patted it, thinking we were lucky to have been left with a little money. I gathered up some wood. I broke sticks and, mumbling to myself, struggled to light the fire.

James woke. "Whacha doing?" he asked sleepily.

"Isn't it obvious?"

I got the fire going and put some rice on to boil. James wandered off into the forest for a pee or something, and I sat watching the flames. The warmth felt good. Then after a bit, a small, light object landed on my head. I looked around. Another small something hit me. I looked up. After a third thing hit me, I untangled a couple of deer droppings from my hair. It was spotted deer poop. I must be one of the only kids on the planet to recognise the sultana-like pellets of hares and deer and the boulders left by elephant and rhino.

I heard a cackle behind me and turned to receive a handful of deer pellets full in the face.

"James...you...!" I scrambled to my feet and gave chase, slowing only for a moment to pick up a couple of cricket-ball-sized bits of rhino dung. My aim was good. They shattered on the back of his neck and mostly fell down inside his shirt. While he emptied poop out of his clothes and shook it from his hair, I returned to the rice and sprinkled in some wild curry leaves.

Our dung-fight had disturbed a troop of rhesus monkeys who had been quietly nibbling buds in the trees above us. They grew noisy too and a warm drizzle of wee descended adding monkey wee to the atmosphere—and the rice.

I squatted down to serve out the food and James said, "Here's a new kind of deodorant for you." And he massaged something damp and sticky into the back of my neck while bits of brown stuff fell into the rice. I was so hungry I didn't care. I just mumbled through the food, "You ungrateful little maggot."

The rice didn't taste of much—not even of deer dung or monkey wee—but it did fill us up. As soon as we'd finished eating, we kicked sand into the fire to put it out.

"C'mon, James, let's get moving."

"Which way?" James was sure it was away from the rising sun.

"We need to walk north-west. I reckon the kidnappers

must've headed into the Chisapaani* Gorge. They'll go up into the mountains from there. But we've got to move fast. Once they've got through the gorge and into the foothills, they could go anywhere, and up there we won't get any help from the police or the army."

After several hot hours of walking—I could only guess how long because the kidnappers had my watch—I started to wonder whether we'd find anywhere recognisable, or anywhere we could get something to drink. We just had to keep going. I heard alarm barks from spotted deer again. Were they scared of us, or was there a tiger or leopard about?

But then, "Hey! Look out!" I shouted at James. My warning came too late.

He had walked right into a huge spider's web. It was strung between two clumps of giant bamboo: about a metre across.

"What the..." He tried to flight the web off, away from his face, pulling bits off his hands and arms.

I shouted, "Look out! Careful—the spider..."

As James struggled, a large yellow-and-black beast came closer to James' face, and I was sure that the spider didn't like what James was doing to her handiwork. James froze and focussed—crossed eyed—on the spider. It was a few centimetres from his nose. I didn't think that this orb spider would hurt him, but I hate spiders. And there was this information in my head that said all spiders are venomous, and whether they can harm you or not has to do with the size of their jaws. This one had big jaws. I had to do something.

I broke off a couple of big leaves and advanced towards James. I put one between the spider and James' face and

63

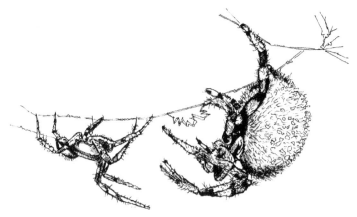

*"James walked right into a huge spider's web strung
between two clumps of giant bamboo"*

tried to wind the web away from him—like rolling spaghetti onto a fork. James bolted. Then I heard a frightened little squeak from him. He'd stopped again.

I caught up with him. There was a much smaller spider— the male—actually on his face. Very close to his eye. I stood for a moment in absolute horror. He didn't look happy either. I broke off another leaf. I put it on James' face close to the spider. The spider walked away from the leaf and closer to James' eye. I moved the leaf. The spider walked towards it. It seemed to smell the leaf, because it waved its feelers at it. The spider was small, but its mouth parts were really big.

"Is it on the leaf yet, Alex?" James whispered.

"Hold still... a bit longer."

The spider didn't move. We didn't move. It waggled its feelers again. It crawled forward so that its front four feet were on the leaf. It stopped and felt around some more. Six feet were on the leaf, then eight. I started, ever so slowly, to pull the leaf away from James' face. Ever so slowly the web pulled the spider off the leaf. Four of its legs were back on his face again.

I returned the leaf to his face. The spider didn't move. I wanted to shove the spider from behind, but I didn't have a stick to poke it with, and I wasn't going to use my finger. I wondered if I dared try to crush the spider, but I knew if I messed up, it might bite James. I never like killing things anyway—not even spiders. Maybe it sensed what I was thinking because all of a sudden it just ran. Right across James' face. It found a strand of web that led back to the bamboo and disappeared.

James mumbled, "Suppose it is sometimes useful to have a bossy big brother."

I looked at him. "Is that you saying thanks?"

"Yeah." He wasn't looking at me. He was concentrating on picking off the last few bits of the sticky web off his face. I considered punching him, but decided I couldn't be bothered.

James said, "I wish I had a gun. Then we could shoot a deer and eat it."

"I know. Food would be good, though I'm not sure I could eat a deer," I said.

"I could!"

"No surprises there then, James."

"Ramdin says there are too many Spotted Deer here in the National Park. They run out of food in the dry season and die in epidemics. He says some should be shot. The meat would help the local villagers through the difficult seasons."

"Yeah, well, Ramdin is probably right, but it is illegal to shoot anything in the park."

"I know, but people do, don't they?"

"Yeah, when they're hungry. Hey, but I heard that if the local Maoists hear gunfire, they take away the weapon for their 'Revolution.'"

"What's Maoists?"

"A group that opposes the government and wants to take over through force. For the moment, though, they seem to have reduced illegal hunting in the park. Whatever, I wish we knew how to find some roots or something we could eat."

A little later, I heard squawks and I looked up to see loads of black-and-white mynah birds squabbling over red fleshy flowers high above us. One fell with a thud that sounded like a cabbage hitting the ground. This was a huge, big-buttressed tree. "This is good news, James!"

"What now?"

"These silk-cotton trees grow close to rivers."

"Who cares?"

"Listen, will you! Can you hear it?"

"What?"

"Moving water."

"What are you on about now, Alex?"

Only a few more metres and we'd arrived. Without a word James walked into the river and knelt to drink. The filth on him muddied the water. He started scrubbing all the rhino dung from his clothes, hair, and skin.

I sort of fell in. The cold took my breath away, but it was a delicious shock. I lay on my front gulping down water. We wallowed and drank more, then just sat on big pebbles in the clear shimmering water.

"Hey, that's Rajapur* Island," I said, pointing. "Look, we've got to get across and then we'll be able to pick up the passenger ferry that'll take us on to Chisapaani. It's pretty close."

"It doesn't look close."

"Yeah, it is, and look, there's the bridge spanning the

66

Chisapaani Gorge!"

James shaded his eyes to look upstream. "But we've got to cross the river to get onto the island, and then it's still a long walk."

"Come on. This looks like a good crossing point. We can wade and swim across here. It's not far."

"I dunno. What is it, 100 metres? A hundred and fifty? I'm not as good as swimming as you, Alex, and there are mugger crocodiles."

"They're not dangerous."

"Maybe, but what about Dad's story of that man who was eaten by one in Sri Lanka? Remember? He said that some of the man's bones and his wedding ring were cut out of the croc's stomach by people from the man's village. The man's wife showed Dad."

I wished he hadn't reminded me of that. I said, "I expect Nepali crocs are different. Ramdin says that muggers aren't dangerous... I'm sure he knows." I wasn't really sure. Mugger mouths look just as big as Nile crocodiles' and those big ugly Australian salties'. "Let's pack everything into my backpack, I'll carry that, and we'll try to cross. We can swim back if it's too far or too deep."

James looked unenthusiastic.

We waded in at a place where the river-smoothed cobblestones showed through shallow rapids. They were all kinds of colours. The sparkling water only came half way to our knees, but already the current made us unsteady and our feet slipped. It would be okay though. It looked quite shallow.

Three-quarters of the way across, the current was much stronger. It was getting seriously difficult. It was up to James' chest, and he thrashed about wildly as he tried to keep on his feet. Each time he slipped, the river swept him further and further downstream, and further and further from me. I tried awkwardly to make my way over to help him get his feet down again, but I was beginning to struggle too.

Upstream I saw two ugly lumps on the river-bank. They lazily slid into the water and disappeared with hardly a ripple. We wouldn't see them even if they came close—until it was too late.

"Swim for it now, James! It's not far..."

The bag weighed me down. I wasn't so confident any more. I didn't know how much I could help James. He plunged forward. The current caught him and swept him away. He was splashing, but afloat. I couldn't believe how quickly the river was taking him.

James went under, and reappeared way downstream. He was spluttering and choking. He went down again and didn't come up.

Then the river swept me off my feet. Something gashed at my leg. It had got a hold of my back-pack and was pulling me under and spinning me. I tumbled over, underwater. My head hit the bottom. I got my feet down and pushed up for the surface. I grabbed a breath and was pulled down again and rolled over. I wasn't sure what was up and what was down. I was sure that it wasn't just the weight of the pack that was pulling me under.

I didn't want to die—not like this.

I stretched out to dry myself in the sun, too. It felt so good on my goose-pimpled skin. The gash in my shin wasn't bleeding much any more.

We must have dozed a bit, because next time I checked, our clothes were dry. I didn't feel sick any more. Hunger made us move on. As we were getting dressed, I noticed vultures circling. Vultures mean a body. Why would anything—or anyone—be dead up here in this remote part of the island?

"Come on James. Let's walk upstream and see what's died."

"Why?"

"Let's just see." I said as we wandered across an expanse of dry cobbles.

A sound behind me made me turn. A whirlwind came rushing past, a dust devil looking like an angry spirit—like something alive. James stuck his tongue out at it. It changed direction, and for a moment I thought it might come after us, but on it went.

"You really like pushing your luck, don't you, little brother!" James' reply was to stick his tongue out at me.

As we got closer to the vultures, I got more and more worried. I was trying not to think that the body might be human. I expected to find a dead ox or a buffalo. Both are sacred to the Tharu* locals, so carcasses are just left to rot. This body was smaller than a cow and had no horns. A pack of skinny village guard dogs were squabbling over it.

The dogs heard and smelt us and looked up. Realising that we were outsiders, they were immediately suspicious. The pack leader turned. He was snarling and angry. He barked instructions and all the other dogs gathered behind him. He started to canter towards us. The pack followed. I turned and ran.

71

All I could hear was growling, angry dogs. They thought we'd come to take their stinking prize. The leader was soon close behind me and gaining fast. How could I expect to out-run them? Then there was a yelp from close up, and another. I glanced back. The pack was in confusion.

James was firing rocks at them, hitting his target each time with a joyous *"howsatt!"* Then he shouted to me, "Stand still! Pick up rocks, and pretend you're playing cricket." There was yelp as another of James' rocks made contact with the bony bottom of another mutt. The pack fled. James swaggered over. "You shouldn't let them know you are scared."

"Yeah, right. Thanks." The pack stayed away now that James had shown them he was the alpha male. Even when we approached to take a closer look at the carcass, they only growled half-heartedly. "*Pwahh*—the stink! How can anything eat something that smelly!" James said. The dog-snacks turned out to be another dog—not Mum or Dad. I stood looking at the carcass feeling slightly sick again. I slipped my hands into my trouser pockets and remembered the treat I'd saved for James.

"Hey, I'd forgotten these. I was saving them until we were really hungry, so now seems a good time. Have some."

"Wow. Sultanas! Those look really good." Greedily he took the lot and fired them into his mouth.

Then, "*Aggh*!" He was coughing and spitting and shouting all at the same time. I'd given him dried hare droppings. I arranged a look of innocent concern on my face.

"What's up?"

"You..." and he ran at me and tackled me to the ground.

Once we'd picked ourselves up, we walked on, circling further to the north. I felt something warm dribbling from the gash in my leg. I suppose more dirt had got into it during the fight. It throbbed a bit too, and that wasn't a good sign. What if it festered? A bad leg would slow me down. We didn't need that.

Three women were working in the rice-fields, collecting tiny freshwater crabs and dropping them into baskets on their belts.

"Imagine being so poor that you actually want to eat those!" I said. "But at least that means there must be some houses close by."

We joined a well-used footpath that wound between rosewoods and flat-topped thorny acacia trees. The women came hurrying past us. They beckoned us to follow, but we took no notice. People were always beckoning us so they could get a closer look or feel our blonde hair. They seemed in a rush, though, and anxiously looked north. I looked to where they were looking. Strangely I couldn't see the gorge any more. Instead there was an angry mass of black clouds that spat lightning. Where the gorge had been, there was just a huge, sand-coloured smudge.

"Look, James!" I cried out.

"Doesn't look friendly! What is it?"

"Dust storm. A big one. We need to find some cover."

"Let's follow those women," James suggested.

"No time!"

"But there's nowhere!" As James said that, the pack of village dogs came cantering past us in tight formation—going fast along the path. They knew where to find shelter.

"Let's see if we can find a hollow somewhere."

The wind blew stronger and stronger, hotter and hotter.

"It feels like someone's opened a huge oven door!"

"Yeah. Let's lie down here, James. Curl up beside me and pull your shirt up over your face." I continued talking in case he was scared, but the noise was terrific, and I don't suppose he could hear me.

The storm hit. It blasted the strip of bare skin above the waistband of my jeans so it stung. It really hurt my leg, too. Sand got into our mouths, into our eyes. It went up our noses making us sneeze. It was so hot that it was hard to breathe. We lay there, eyes clamped shut, ears singing. All we could do is wait. Lying face down in the dirt, I was thinking about my cousins back in England. They were forever on about what an amazing life we had, living in the foothills of the Himalayas. We did have an amazing life, but not always in a good way. Nature could really show you who was in charge—who had the power.

Then as suddenly as it had started, the wind dropped. Big blood-warm drops of rain fell. It made spots in the dust on James' face so he looked as if he'd caught some horrible disease. Then it poured. We stood with our mouths open to catch some rain and wash out the grit. The downpour cleared the air, and as it eased I spotted something good. "Look, James—over there. It's one of those towers people build to keep a look out for elephants. That must be a village."

As we walked closer, we saw a couple of huts in the distance. This, we hoped, was where we'd find the ferry.

Soon we came to a tiny ram-shackled tea shop. I was pleased to see a line of big round unglazed clay pots outside, containing delicious cool water. There was a pet rhesus monkey tied up outside. Smoke seeped through the thatch; the cooking fire was lit. We'd be able to buy tea, and there might even be food. All the women and girls were bustling about their work. Some were washing away the dust before cutting vegetables, some sorted rice, some were splitting wood and others were pounding clothes clean with smooth rocks from the river.

Inside the tea shop, the atmosphere was so thick it stung our eyes. People were shouting orders for tea and food.

I asked a woman, "Can we take the boat to Chisapaani from here?"

"It is possible," she said. "After the ferryman has eaten rice." Then she started to laugh at us. "Were you out in that sandstorm, boys?"

"We were, and we're hungry—and thirsty! Can we eat?"

"You can eat—if you like chillies?"

"Yes, we do."

While she was serving the rice, she rambled on about how we were lucky to have any rice, since elephants had come across from the reserve and eaten most of last season's harvest. It nearly all went in one night, despite them keeping look out and despite lighting fires to scare the elephants away.

I managed to butt in and ask, "Have you seen two other foreigners—a man and a woman?"

"Two *Angrez* crossed on the ferry two hours ago—with some men from the hills."

I turned to James, "They're only two hours ahead!"

"That's a lot," he said, sounding tired.

"Are you seeking someone, little *sahibs*?*"

We hadn't noticed anyone else, so it was spooky to hear a voice coming out of a dark corner. When our eyes had adjusted to the gloom we saw an old man. He wore a soft colourful *topi** on his greying head and his fine white moustache was waxed into a point on each side of his mouth. He continued, "Sergeant Tek Bahadhur Rai—of the Gurkha* Regiment—at your service. Is your family also coming?"

"They're ahead," I said wanting to tell him as little as possible, especially as I was too hungry for conversation. We joined him at his table anyway, thinking he'd probably do most of the talking.

"Oh, hey," James interrupted, wanting to return to the most important subject of food, "There's yoghurt!" He turned to the owner of the tea shop and asked her for some. A few minutes later she came back inside carrying yoghurt and three brown cakes. James was about to ask for one, when he recognised them as dried cow dung—to fuel the cooking fire.

There was a portrait of Ganesh pinned to the wall, and in front of him was a small table where an oil lamp burned. Tek Bahadhur must have been staring at me because he started up the conversation again. "This is Lord Ganesh. He is most popular of all our Hindu gods." He was talking down to us—like we were tourists.

"Mmm," I said through a big mouthful of rice. "We like him, too. He looks so friendly with his elephant trunk, smiley face, and big fat stomach!"

"Do you know how he got his elephant's head?"

"No." I said knowing that Nepalis are great story-tellers and it would keep him from asking us questions. "Do tell us."

"Lord Ganesh is the most popular god because he is solving all kinds of problems for us. Without the blessing and grace of Sri Ganesh, nothing can be achieved. It is necessary to bring offerings to him before starting any new undertaking. He has the power to take away obstacles, but also he can place obstacles in the way of the unworthy."

James and I exchanged glances. I made a mental note to at least give Ganesh a nod on the way out.

"He is the son of the beautiful Parbati, but she gave birth to Ganesh while her husband—Lord Shiva—was away at war. Their son grew up and did his duty in protecting the honour of his mother while her husband was busy. Then after many years Shiva came home from the wars. Father and son didn't recognise each other. Ganesh challenged him, so Shiva cut off Ganesh's head. Parbati was upset and cried and cried that her only son was dead. Wanting to make his wife happy again, Shiva promised to give Ganesh a new head—from the next living thing that passed by. That happened to be an elephant, so Shiva cut off its head, placed it on Ganesh, and breathed life back into him.

"In many temples, you will see our holy family, with Lord Ganesh, with his elephant head, sitting smiling on Parbati's lap."

"Nice story. Thanks, Mr. Rai."

"It is my privilege and pleasure and my duty also... "

James said, "I liked that, too, but think what would have happened if the next living thing to pass by had been a worm—with no eyes and their heads all mouth and slime."

I wished James would shut up.

"Now tell me where you are going, boys. Tell me why your parents are not with you!"

I didn't want to answer, but I didn't want to be rude either. "Birdwatching!" I blurted out. "You see lots more birds if you travel in small groups... And where are *you* going today?"

"Kathmandu. I am going to take the overnight bus..."

I nodded to James. "We are heading that way, too."

As we left, I placed a shiny one rupee coin in front of the image of Ganesh, and the three of us wandered down to the river. There, we scrambled into the dugout ferry and squatted down, but tutting, the ferryman told to us sit in the puddle in the bottom of the dugout.

Once everyone was on board, he shoved off. The boat wobbled alarmingly, but he paddled us calmly northwards. Looking at the water surface as it whizzed by made me feel dizzy, so instead I concentrated on looking into the puddle between my knees. It was good that we were getting even closer to the deep gash in the foothills that is the Chisapaani Gorge.

Tek Bahadhur prattled on, but now we didn't have to pretend we were listening to him.

Finally, there was a grinding sound as the boat ran up onto a stony beach. We scrambled out gratefully, unsticking wet trousers from our bums as we paid our two rupee fares to the ferryman.

"Go with good fortune, little-*sahibs*," Tek Bahadhur shouted in his commanding voice, and then, at surprising speed for an old man, he quick-marched towards the bridge, where the buses waited.

"*Pheri betaw la**, then," I said.

He waved without looking back.

10
THE GORGE

The tea shop on the island had seemed busy, but the bazaar at the mouth of the gorge was ear-splitting with screechy Hindi film music, thumping generators, blacksmiths hammering, motorbikes revving, children crying, women shouting, piglets squealing, sows grunting, dogs yelping and cockerels crowing. Despite the noise a man was stretched out fast asleep in the sun. Three boys shouted, "Hey, *queeries*!*" And ran away laughing, delighted to have been a little rude to us light-skinned outsiders.

The smell of roasting peanuts made my mouth water but I couldn't see the seller. James stopped and looked longingly at a stall selling green orange and pink plastic weapons, and then he spotted a sweet stall.

"Hey, look—*laddoos** and *jelabis*!*"

A well-fed rat chased by a skinny, grey cat shot out from under the stall. The cat's fur was matted into tufts. The hunter and the hunted dashed between the stalls and disappeared over the steep edge of the road. I looked to see where they'd gone to. It was a long way down to the river. At the water's edge below, skinny children picked around looking for anything useful or attractive amongst the stuff people threw down there. I thought about the orphan rag-picker who worked the rubbish heap just along the road from where we lived in Kathmandu. He slept on the street and although he was about James' age he was tiny: the size of a six-year-old. His hair was all matted—like that cat's—I guess he had nowhere to wash. He used a bent bicycle spoke as a hook and pulled out meat bones to sell to the glue factory in Kumbeswar and plastic bags to sell somewhere else. He was always grinning and called us, "my *Angrez* brothers."

He'd been a bit bewildered when they moved his particular rubbish heap. People used to throw stuff at the corner of our road, but neighbours had collected money to build a small shrine, our shrine, to pot-bellied Ganesh. There was a bell, to wake up the elephant-headed god when you wanted to ask him for something. Lots of people visited and people couldn't dump rubbish there any more. Instead they lit butter lamps and sprinkled red petals and scented water around the god to welcome each new day. It always smelt nice.

"Alex?"

"Yeah?"

"These sweets look good."

"Do you *ever* think about anything but your stomach?"

"No—why should I?"

The sweets stall-holder whisked flies off his treasures. I imagined biting into a syrup-filled *jelabi* and the syrup exploding into my mouth. The thought of it made me feel dreamy again, but, I shook my head, "Come on. Not now.

80

We've got to find Mum and Dad."

"A samosa then," he said gazing hopefully into huge wok of boiling oil. I couldn't resist. That stall-holder fired four into a paper bag made out of someone's school maths worksheet. James gobbled his down, while I savoured the delicious tingling in my mouth from the spices.

The bazaar was seething with people, but we knew none of them. It's weird how you can feel so lonely in a crowd.

"Alex... ALEX!"

"Yeah?"

"Isn't that Ramdin over there?"

"As in... Dad's field assistant?"

"Yeah—look."

"Looks like him—come on. He might know something."

We tried to push forward but there were so many people it was difficult getting to him. By the time we got close, he was walking away. We lost sight of him and weren't even sure if it had been him. There was no reason for him to be in Chisapaani.

Then a man I didn't know walked up to us and kind of blocked our way. We looked at each other. It seemed strange that he didn't offer a greeting. Then he spoke. "You Flaming boys should get on the bus. Go straight. Go back to Kathmandu. If you try to go north the situation will become messy. You understand?"

I might have nodded slightly. There was something about this man that really frightened me. He was used to being obeyed. A bulging in his pocked said he was armed. He turned and he too disappeared into the crowds. I looked to see what James thought about this "advice" and realised—with a jolt— that he wasn't there. I had no idea where my exasperating brat of a kid brother had gone to. He couldn't have been listening to that last conversation. He seemed to have just wandered off. I looked for him, expecting him to have gone back to the *jelabi* stall, but eventually I found him with a group of kids playing *chungi*. James was trying to kick a bit of rolled up bicycle inner-tubing without letting it hit the ground. He managed four kicks. The Nepali kids laughed at his incompetence. Even the littlest can kick it a hundred times without letting it fall. James wandered back to me looking fed up. "I wish I was better at *chungi*."

"It's not exactly the time to be practising, is it! WE NEED TO KEEP GOING. He opened his mouth to speak when a girl ran straight into me, "*Maaf**, *dai**!" she said apologetically.

"What the –"

She was much shorter than me but probably about my age. At first she avoided looking directly at us, like low caste people do, but then I saw she was shyly glancing from me to James and back again.

"Alek! Chimes! *Mero** *sati haru**! What are you doing here?" She was grinning now. Her eyes sparkled as she looked directly at us. She looked from me to James.

"Wow! *Atti-bahini**! Good to see you. Great to see a friendly face!" We'd grown up with her in Rajapur. She'd always seemed ill when she was tiny, and her mother dressed her in her brothers' hand-me-down trousers. Now, though, she'd grown her hair and wore a fashionable *shalwar kameez*. She'd become a woman while we'd been away, and she was beautiful. "What are *you* doing here?"

"I was shopping only, but –" she looked around. "I am sooo happy to see you." She grabbed my arm. "A man tried to catch

82

me and pull me somewhere at the backside of the stalls over there. I bit him, and he let go. Then I ran and found you. This is fully good *karma**, no?"

She still looked scared. I couldn't think what to say so I offered her a samosa. We ate as I told her the bones of our story. Her eyes widened and she looked more and more horrified as the details came out.

"These are dangerous men also, my friends. I must tell my father. I will telephone him—at the police headquarters."

"No—I think if anyone knows—even the police—our parents will be in greater danger. This has to be our secret."

"It is as you wish, but I must come with you. I will call my father—so he doesn't worry. But I shall hint a little at the problem so he can make some discreet enquiries. He understands these things. He does not trust his superiors also."

I didn't know what to say. I knew Atti could be a huge help to us, and I really, really didn't want to do this on my own, but…

"Surely—after what's just happened—you'd best not get involved, Atti. It is too dangerous."

"You, my friends, have no idea how dangerous this is! That is why I must go with you this day."

There was—apparently—no arguing with her. Girls can be like that.

She raised her hand and said, "*Ekk chin ma*" and spoke to a stall-holder who handed her a plastic jug full of water. She poured some into her mouth without her lips touching the jug and drank down a lot of water. She handed the jug to me. "Drink!"

I felt a bit embarrassed as I gave the jug back to the stall-holder without taking a drink. I wasn't that worried about the

83

quality of the water, but I knew I'd pour it all down my front if I tried to drink in the correct way. Hindus really mind about this stuff. They won't drink from a shared cup, and I didn't want to upset anyone. I rummaged in my bag and drank from my water bottle. James did the same. Atti showed us a water pump where we could refill them, and then we set off together.

A wide dirt road cut through the middle of the bazaar, but so few vehicles or even ox carts came this way that various goods and the stall-holders' cloth sunshades were stretched right across the road. As we were finishing the samosas, a four-wheel-drive Toyota pickup arrived with its horn blaring. The driver clearly intended to drive though—market or not. The stall-holders hastily moved pots and boxes and untied their awnings to let this Big Man by.

"Inspector-*sahib*," I heard Atti whisper; this was the local police chief. "It is better he does not see us." She stepped back and melted into the background as if by magic.

The car stopped.

"Try to look cute will you, Chimes!" I said. "It would be good to find out what he knows about the kidnappers."

"Bog off!" James pouted. "And don't call me Chimes, Alek."

The important men in the car scowled at us. Unlike most Nepalis, they weren't at all friendly. They didn't stop to talk. People in the market were trying to catch the big man's attention too, as if they were trying to tell him something, but he didn't want to know. Perhaps he'd had a tip-off and was intent only on chasing the kidnappers.

Then something odd happened. A man stepped out of the crowd and approached the Toyota pickup. The man looked like Tek Bahadur. He talked to the Chief Inspector

84

like they were best mates. The man turned, and I saw it *was* Tek Bahadur. He hadn't caught the bus. He'd lied to us. He turned for a moment, and we looked at each other. I expected him to come over and speak to us, but he turned back to finish his conversation with the Chief Inspector. Then another man approached the Toyota pickup. It was Ramdin. This time I was sure it was him. The three of them talked briefly, then turned away and were quickly lost in the crowd.

"I have a horrible feeling there's a lot more going on than we know about. Come on, James. Let's buy some biscuits to keep us going. We've got some serious walking to do."

"Yeah, okay, but look at your leg! It looks bad," he said.

My trousers were blood-stained and blood continued to dribble into my sock. "It's fine."

"You should strap it up or something."

"It's okay. Let's go."

Atti reappeared. "I have *chura!*" She held a big bag of pounded rice flakes and a smaller bag of raisins.

"Great thinking Atti—good to nibble as we walk."

As she led us north, she said, "We must be careful. It is better you tell people you are tourists on holiday..."

"Atti?"

"*Hunchha**, Alek *dai?*"

"We met someone waiting for the ferry. He asked all sorts of questions. He was quite pushy. It wasn't like the usual chat. I just saw him talking to the Chief Inspector. It was almost as if he was spying on us, and reporting to him. Is that likely?"

"It is possible, Alek. People are saying the Secret Police are coming back. We must be most careful who we talk to ...and trust no one."

"Yeah, I know."

"What did this man look like, Alek?"

"Grey hair. Amazing moustache waxed to two points; military. Ex-Gurkha. Why?"

"That was the very man who frightened me in the bazaar."

I didn't know what to say. What *had* we got into? A dreadful thought struck me: if high-level police were involved, our parents must be in great danger. I felt ill again, wishing I could think of something more cheerful.

We walked in silence into the calm shade and the vivid greenness of the gorge. The main path was five metres above the clear cool river, which had carved the white limestone into smooth curves and coves. After the parching heat out on the Plains, it felt good. The gorge walls were almost vertical, but even so, high above us, there were trees growing out of the sheer rock face. The cliffs seemed impossibly high, sharp, and threatening.

James pointed down to a whirlpool. "Wouldn't it be cool to get sucked down deep under the water—I wonder where you'd end up? Maybe in some cave—with treasure."

Atti just shook her head. I pitied my baby brother. He was so not-on-this-planet sometimes.

The path was flat and wide. We strode along at a good pace. The sounds of birds calling and the soothing music of the rushing river made the place feel friendly, until a flock of dull-looking brown babblers landed, noisily, just up ahead. A fight broke out. One of the seven ended up standing on another bird's head, pecking him mercilessly. Up above, a troop of ivory-white langurs looked down disapprovingly, their long bell-pull tails moving slightly in the breeze.

Atti, smiling, pouted towards a sound in the undergrowth. I like the way Nepalis point by pouting their lips; they reckon pointing with a finger is rude.

Three mongooses, playing chase, burst out of the undergrowth and came galumphing across the track. The leader stopped and the other two bounced on him. There was a crazy bundle of squealing fur, ears, noses and tails. The mongooses broke apart. All three stood up on hind legs to look at us.

She whispered, "I will tell you one story about the mongooses. It is most strange, but the Lord Ratnasambhava keeps all his treasure inside the mongooses. When the god needs his gems and jewels, he squeezes one mongoose and makes it vomit them up!"

"Charming!"

James said, "Shall I grab one, squeeze it, and get the jewels?"

"In your dreams."

We kept on staring at the mongooses, which were staring at us. As soon as James took one step towards them, though,

"The Lord Ratnasambhava keeps his treasure inside the mongooses"

they decided that we *were* frightening and scampered away.

I was about to say something when Atti held up her hand for silence. I listened too and made out a deep noise, like distant thunder. I thought about landslides and earthquakes. We'd often felt tremors. There have been really big earthquakes in the Himalayas and people in Kathmandu talk all the time about when others will come. How dangerous would one be here and now? The cliffs all around us could easily come crashing down.

We listened some more. The earth wasn't moving. The sound grew louder and louder. The police chief's jeep was coming—fast. When they saw us, they hit the horn and we had to jump into the undergrowth to get off the track. Now we were choking, blinded, and eating dust.

"They were in a hurry," James gasped.

"Yeah. They didn't seem to care if they killed us either."

Half a mile further on, we discovered why the jeep had turned back. The road had fallen away. The river had gobbled up all the forest and scree, so it was now just sheer walls and water. Looking downstream, I could see the destruction. Each side of the gorge was splattered with bits of trees that looked as if a giant had munched them up and spat them out.

"Remember the thunder we heard a couple of nights ago? There must have been one of those flash floods that I've heard Dad talking about—when water comes powering down from the mountains... so... what do we do now?"

I turned to see Atti was now facing the river. Oddly, she shouted in Nepali, "Hey! Brother!" I looked in the direction she was facing and saw she was addressing someone on the other side of the river. I realised—because the man was walking along it—that there was another path. The traveller wore jodhpurs, a double-breasted shirt, and a colourful cloth hat, small enough to cover his bald spot. His only luggage was a radio; he was listening to screechy songs from Hindi films.

"Greetings boys, sister. All right?" he shouted back.

"We're well. You also?" (Even when shouting across a river, you had to do this polite stuff first.)

"Where are you going?" Atti asked.

"Up to my village."

"Can we cross the river and get onto the path you are on, brother?"

"It is not possible. You must go back to the bridge at Chisapaani. There is no other bridge."

"Is there no other way?"

"There is a small, small goat track above you. Look up and you can see it, but only Nepali people can use it. You cannot take those *Angrez* boys across. It is too dangerous for them. You must go back."

"We can't. We must go on—quickly," she replied.

"Go back, little sister."

"We are trying to find our parents," I butted in.

"I saw a man and a woman with some strangers from the hills earlier. The foreigners did not look happy."

"Where did you see them?" I asked.

"They are on this side of the river. Not far ahead. If you try the path you could cross in a boat at my village... It is better that you get help. You must inform the police."

"The police will do nothing."

"It is true, boys. What can we do in the face of all the bad men in the world?"

He walked on—north. I wanted to apologise to Atti. Her father was a policeman, but he was a good, honest policeman. She looked at me and smiled as if she knew what I was thinking.

We looked up at the goat track. "So let's do some climbing!" James said.

"The man said that it was too difficult," I argued.

"Yeah, but Nepalis think that all foreigners are useless at climbing, or even walking."

Atti nodded in agreement.

James said, "Let's just go for it!"

Atti frowned, shook her head, but took off her flip-flops and turned to lead the way. Clumsily, we followed. She moved noiselessly up through undergrowth that grew out of loose stony red soil. We knocked rocks down. When we were about 15 metres above the path, we reached the tiny track. Lots of small loose stones covered it, making it easy to slip.

"Shall we go for it then?"

"Yup. It looks okay to me," James said. I wished I had his confidence. I was feeling really, really nervous about this climb already. I'm scared of heights. It is annoying. I hate it, but as Nepalis often say helplessly, "What can I do?"

Atti was already striding confidently along the path. She was soon around a corner and out of sight.

At first the going was reasonably easy, but the track quickly narrowed so there wasn't room to place two feet side-by-side. The path climbed and the gorge-sides became much steeper. We were going very slowly and carefully now. James was ahead of me. He shouted back, "You won't like this, Alex. Don't look down."

I was sick of his pointless advice. I swore at him under my breath. I dared not shout. I needed to concentrate on where I was putting my feet. Looking down made me aware of how far we might fall. The swirling water below made my head spin. My knees started to tremble. I found a ledge to cling on to. It was covered in bird lime.

"Just shuffle along. It gets wider soon."

I focussed on the cliff wall on my left. There were fossil shells and coral in the rock. I took some breaths and calmed myself.

"Keep going," James said. "It's really not too bad. Just keep going."

He turned, meaning to go on.

"*Ahhh!*" He'd stood on a loose stone and slipped. Everything went into slow motion. His hand lashed out. He made a grab for the cliff wall. There were no hand-holds.

For a moment he balanced on one leg, then that foot slipped off as well. I wanted to lunge forward and catch him, but he was too far away. I nearly toppled off as well.

He started to fall. He flung out one arm and grabbed onto a thin spike of limestone. He clung there. He scrabbled until his feet found a tiny ledge, and he started to climb back up. For a moment he looked as if he'd mange to get onto the ledge again.

I edged forward to help him, but there was a fearful *CRACK*. The spike that he was clinging on to broke. James fell twenty metres to the river below. There were two big splashes, as my brother and the rock hit the water. They both disappeared without a trace.

"JAMES—NOOO!" I shouted.

Then I did a totally mad thing. I jumped in after him.

"A Black-naped Hare had come down to the river to drink"

11
BEST MEDICINE

I hit the water. My muscles seized with the stabbing cold. I went down deep. I was churned and tossed and battered by the river, like I was inside a washing machine. The backpack was pulling me down. I couldn't breathe. I couldn't get up to the air. I tore off the backpack. Once free, I struggled up to the surface. Now my clothes were attacking me. My shirt was in my face. The current kept me down. I fought my way up. Grabbed a breath. It was foam not air. The stuff I breathed in made me choke. I was under again, coughing. Trying not to cough.

Desperately, I swam up to air, gasped for a couple of seconds and was pulled back under. I don't know how many times I was sucked down and thrashed my way back up. Just as I thought my lungs would burst, I got to the surface. I grabbed half a breath before yet another eddy pulled me down.

I was starting to weaken. How many more times could I fight my way to the air?

Finally the river calmed. I surfaced. I took several breaths. The current spun me like a dancer, but it had finished playing with me. Suddenly, unexpectedly, there was sand under my feet. I stumbled and crawled out and collapsed on a small beach. I lay there gasping. Choking. Shivering.

When I gathered enough strength to sit up, I saw that I was on a small sandbank. It smelt of fish. There were footprints and marks where large reptiles had squirmed out to bask in the sun. The back of my neck tingled as I realised that this beach belonged to crocodiles. I stood up unsteadily and looked around. What about James? Was he okay? Had he managed to escape the strange river currents? And Atti? Where was she?

I was—at least—on the right side, the east side, of the river now. This was where our parents had walked so recently. That cheered me. It was an easy scramble up to a narrow but well-used path. I stood wondering what to do. Which way should I go? Then I saw a very wet James striding towards me. "You all right?" I asked.

"Yeah. The gorge wall was so sheer I fell straight into the water and the current dumped me on a bit of a beach down there. I think Atti would say that we have good *karma* today. Are YOU all right?"

"I think so—a bit dazed," I stammered.

"You look awful. Did you fall, too?"

"No, I jumped."

"Why?"

"Thought I might be able to help you."

"Really?"

"Yeah, but the current was too strong, and my backpack

is at the bottom of the river. It was dragging me under."

"Wow. Really?" Then he said, "Where's Atti?"

"Dunno—but she'll be okay. I suppose she'll just walk back down to Rajapur now we've been separated. I hope she doesn't say too much. I hope she doesn't tell Arjun too much, or call out the Army or anything silly. We'd better hurry on whatever...."

"Yeah, better get going."

Then my mouth went watery and I puked.

James looked at the mess. "Thanks for that. *Aggh*, you got my shoes!"

We walked on. James was quieter than usual. We didn't talk for ages; we were lulled into a kind of trance by the rhythm of putting one foot in front of the other, allowing all that had happened to soak into our tired brains.

When I next glanced up, the gorge walls weren't so extreme. They weren't so steep and high. The valley was widening out. The river was broader, shallower, and slower moving. There were a few small fields now, chickens everywhere and buildings that were very different to the flimsy low huts that we'd left behind on the Plains. There were wooden houses, some on two storeys.

I was hoping the walk would help settle my jitters, but I couldn't get rid of the feeling that something awful was about to happen. It seemed stupid, but it still felt like we were being watched.

James pointed across to a movement in the bushes close to the river bank. "What's that?"

I'd so convinced myself someone was watching, I was completely panicked. I was about to run for it, when I realised it was only a black-naped hare that had come down to drink.

A bit further on, a woman was using bamboo chopsticks to pick nettles. The first time we saw people picking nettles to eat we felt sorry for them, because only the very poor eat nettles, but then we'd got a taste for them and—to Laxmi's deep disapproval—Mum cooked them for us sometimes.

"Hey look! That tea shop up ahead might serve some food," I said.

"Awesome. Look—there's cooking smoke coming through the roof-slats. We should be able to buy some sweet tea, at least. I love that stuff."

"Mmm. This must be the village that the man in the gorge talked about." A rough dugout canoe was pulled up on the beach beneath the path. "There—that's the ferry."

We approached the tiny shack, took off our shoes, and put them in a patch of sun to dry them out a bit. Then we ducked inside. We were greeted by a rich fudgy smell. I was ravenous again.

"You took your time!" Atti was inside—smiling broadly. The woman who owned the little shop also gave us a gappy-toothed grin. Her face was the colour of an old flowerpot, but polished and shiny. Her sun-scorched cheekbones were the colour of new brick.

She said, "I have been waiting for you, little *sahibs*." She beckoned us to sit, while she blew into the fire to heat up the tea. She didn't allow us to get a word in as she chatted, about the path, about the fish in the river, and the weather we should expect. Meanwhile, our clothes gently steamed dry.

Atti said, "So, James, you found a nice whirlpool to jump into. Did you find a cave at the bottom?"

James just grunted, "Weren't you worried about us?"

"No – I knew you were safe." Atti didn't have much else to say to us, but we were pleased to be back together. Tea and Glucose biscuits further cheered the three of us. The tea-shop was small and cosy. A butter lamp illuminated a tiny cheap statue of Ganesh in a slot in the wall.

After a while, Atti said, "I must tell you one thing, Alek."

"What's that?"

"The man you spoke of—the Gurkha who seemed to be spying on you?"

"Yeah?"

"I am fully sure now, Alek. He was the one who tried to catch hold of me in the bazaar. It think he wanted to traffic me."

"But you're only –"

James said, "What's traffic got to do with anything?"

"I'll tell you later."

"That's what Mum says when she thinks I'm too young to hear stuff."

"You *are* too young, Little Chimes," Atti said.

He looked ready to explode.

"Listen, cool it, James, this is important—let's hear what Atti has to say." I threw him another packet of Glucose biscuits, like throwing fish to a penguin in the zoo.

She took a breath, "I saw this man. On this path. I think he *is* following me—or you!"

The tea shop owner seemed interested, especially when I'd said Gurkha, but she didn't know much English.

"What are we going to do, Atti?"

"I will speak to the tea shop owner. Maybe she will help us."

I thought I'd better break a slightly strained silence that followed as we all worried about what to do next. "The doorway of this hut is very low. It must be a real pain, because even the tea shop owner has to stoop down to get in and out. Why have they built it like this?"

"It is necessary—to keep out ghosts," Atti explained, without explaining a thing.

"Ghosts?"

"She told me, before you arrived, that in her last house there was a big doorway and she had a lot of trouble with ghosts. She prayed to Ganesh for help but, even so, one ghost threw her husband out of the first floor window—in the middle of the night, it was. The ghost was trying to take their maize: the grain that they store up in the roof."

I looked at her face. I couldn't decide if she was teasing or making fun of us.

"Now," Atti continued, "she doesn't have so much trouble. Ghosts can't bend down. Low doorways stop them, unless the ghost has had its head cut off and carries it under its arm. That headless kind can still get in, but there aren't so many of those. This kind is rare."

Ghosts were the least of my worries though. "Did you gather any news of our parents, Atti?"

She looked as if she was going to say something, but then noticed the rip in my trousers and saw my wounded leg. It had been getting hotter and redder and throbbed all the time now.

"This looks bad, Alek!" Atti said something to the tea shop owner. "*Didi** says she has good medicine for this." The tea shop owner produced some foul-looking black sludge smeared onto a piece of old newspaper. She came towards

98

me with her eyes fixed on my sore leg.

"What's that? What are you going to do?"

"This is best medicine, Alek...Don't be scared."

"Yes, don't be scared, Alex," James echoed.

"What is it?" I said, backing away.

"It is from the insides of batteries—very good medicine, it is, *babu**."

I said, "Maybe I can find a clinic and get treatment there instead. Don't you ever go to the government clinic, *didi*?"

"No, *babu*. They know nothing there—and they charge too much money."

"It is fine, Alek—just let her do this thing!" Atti's expression said—not for the first time—that she was tired of my fussing.

I had an idea that batteries were full of poisonous acids and heavy metals and stuff, but I also knew that soon the leg would start slowing me down, so what choice did I have?

The *didi* squatted in front of me and plastered the black sludge onto my leg. It stung horribly. Then she rubbed it in with her dirt-blackened fingers and made it hurt a lot more. I tried not to let the pain show in my face. I didn't want Atti to think I was a complete wuss.

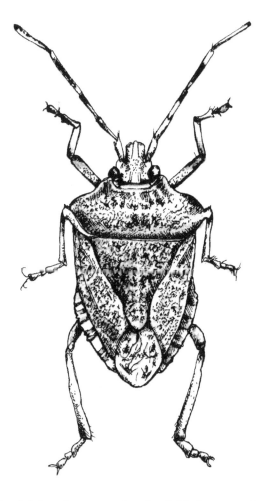

"A stink bug has committed suicide in my tea"

12
STINK BUG

Once the tea shop-owner had finished "healing me," I brought the conversation around to other people she'd seen that day. Our parents had been marched through; they were not far ahead. "Which way did they go, *didi?*" I asked.

"From here there are two paths. The main route follows the river to Achham. They took the other path that climbs high over the ridge and into the wild country. They went into the *jungle.* Not many go that way, except Maoists. You must be careful of them. You must be careful of the spirits of the mountains, too. And bears. Many bad things happen there. Sometimes Lord Shiva becomes angry and he shakes the earth, and there are terrible landslides and avalanches. Many local people go up there to visit the holy cave and make offerings to Lord Shiva. If he receives enough offerings, then maybe he will not grow angry."

"A cave?" James asked.

Atti said, "Yes. Visiting it might improve our *karma*—we'll be sure to free your parents if we make an offering in such a holy place."

"The best time to visit is on Saturday when most people go to worship," the tea shop woman said. "That will be after two days. Here now, drink." We took the steaming hot glasses and sipped the seriously sweet thick tea.

Then James said, "*Aghh*, gross, disgusting!"

"What's up?" I asked.

"A stink bug committed suicide in my tea. Now it tastes foul."

"You have a problem, son?" the old woman asked. When she saw the body floating legs up in the tea, she took his glass, threw the tea out of the glassless window and refilled it. "There are too many of these insects in this season," she complained.

Atti started talking to the *didi* in Nepali so fast I couldn't follow much of what they were saying. There was a lot of laughing. When I gave Atti a quizzical look, she just said in English, "Be a little bit patient, Alek."

When they finally stopped chatting, I said, "Well?"

"I will tell you later—maybe." She was enjoying being annoying.

"Pleeeeease, Atti!" I gave her my best mock-sad eyed look to make her laugh.

"All right, Alek. I asked her to tell the military man that we were planning to take the route to Achham. I gave her a little bit of money also. She was happy."

"Sounds good. I think. Err. So that's NOT the route we plan to take, right?"

"Correct."

We paid for the tea, bought a few more battered-looking packets of biscuits, I found a coin to leave for Ganesh, and we stepped outside. Apparently waiting for us was a familiar figure.

"Ramdin-*dai*! What...?"

"Boys! It is good to see you! What good luck that we have met like this!"

We were dumbstruck.

Then something really weird happened. I felt suddenly a bit unsteady on my feet. There was a strange feeling in my guts like someone was wobbling my belly, but from the inside. Then it felt like someone had grabbed hold of the ground and was pulling it bad-temperedly back and forward. It made me stagger. James almost fell, but then recovered and said, "Wicked—an earthquake!"

The tea shop owner lunged out through her tiny little doorway and stood well clear of her house. The back-and-forward motion didn't go on for long, but it clearly frightened her. She seemed to be mumbling prayers and was frantically looking around at the hillsides and the mountain ridges, checking, I guess, for landslides and rockfalls.

Ramdin hadn't been spooked by it at all. "So will you boys introduce me to your friend here?"

"Oh. Yeah. This is Atti. Um. Er. A friend—as you say. A very old friend."

"Atti only?"

"Atti." I didn't want to mention her father's name. Suddenly I didn't want to tell him anything. He'd been the guy who had taught us so much about the forest. He'd been an amazing guide and font of knowledge. I thought he was a family friend, but now, suddenly, I didn't trust him. I didn't trust him at all.

"So, where are you going, boys?"

"Oh, we decided ages ago..." James was watching me, keeping his mouth shut for a change, "we decided we'd climb up to one of the big caves people go on pilgrimages to..."

"Very good—a pilgrimage."

"So where are *you* going, Ramdin-*dai?*"

"I am going to my village."

"But I thought..." I stopped myself commenting on this lie. "Er, so what about the fieldwork? How's that going?"

"Good—we have found one sloth bear den. We are getting very good data, but your parents suggested I take a break—see my family. Now it is my idea that we will be able to walk together. I know this cave." What the heck was he saying? His family didn't live this way. His wife and children were in Nepalgunj and his mother in Mahendranagar. And he wasn't carrying presents. Nepalis don't go home without presents. "Let us start now, yeah?" he said.

We didn't seem to have much choice without raising suspicion. Not far from the tea shop, the path forked. "We will take the high route, I am thinking?" Ramdin said.

"*Hunchha, dai,*" Atti agreed, but her whole demeanour said she didn't trust Ramdin either. She too was saying as little as possible to him. The valley side was steep here, and she seemed to be searching for something as we climbed. Then suddenly she turned to James and said, "James, my friend, you are looking very tired."

James was about to argue when something inside his slow-moving brain clicked, and he put on a pathetic face. Atti continued, "Let us stop here and take a drink." She pointed to a good sized ledge where a lot of Daphne bushes grew. We would be quite well hidden from people walking along the path. We all four sat, pulled out our water bottles and drank. The scent of the Daphne flowers reached me.

"So tell me about yourself, Atti-*bahini*," Ramdin said.

"Oh, I am far too tired to talk, *dai*."

James opened his mouth then closed it again. I probably pulled a face too. Atti was one of the toughest people I knew. I waited to see if we'd discover why she was being so mysterious.

After a few minutes, Atti started fussing around and whispered, "Take a biscuit, *dai*."

"Biscuits are for children, *bahini*."

Then I looked where Atti was looking and saw an old man with a colourful cloth hat striding along the path. It took a few more moments before I was sure it was Tek Bahadur. We watched him take the lower path—towards Achham. So he *was* following us!

I watched Ramdin follow our gazes. He visibly tensed when he saw Tek Bahadur. For a moment, I think Ramdin considered shouting at him, but when he started to look uncomfortable, I enquired casually, "Someone you know?"

"I do not know this man," Ramdin said.

Okay, so this was an outright lie. I'd seen them talking in the bazaar—today! I wished I could ask Atti what she thought was going on.

Once Tek Bahadur was well out of sight, Atti led us back onto the path and then steeply up over rocky ground. Clouds rolled in, and suddenly it felt cold. A lonely crow called its name, "*Kaag, kaag**."

This was going to be a tough ascent. I thought we'd each

find our comfortable pace, but Atti was soon way head again. Ramdin walked with us. I couldn't decide if he was being sociable or liked our pace because he was old and not very fit. I wondered if I could signal to Atti—so we could talk.

James whinged, "She's walking too fast. You're walking too fast." Then he shouted, "Atti! Let me lead for a while!"

"But you don't know the way," she told him. "And you walk too slowly."

"We're just following the path, aren't we?"

Atti ignored him and forged ahead.

A bit later, James said, "Hey, how about we stop up by that boulder and have a biscuit?"

A breathless Ramdin nodded enthusiastically.

I looked up. There were patches of snow around us. We were quite high already.

"Hey, look at that!" I pointed to the ground as I rummaged for biscuits.

"What is it with you and poop, Alex?"

"It's a carnivore dropping—leopard, I think. Look at all the pieces of broken bone in it!"

"Who cares?" James said.

"We might—if it's still hungry," Ramdin chuckled.

"So where exactly is your house, Ramdin?" I asked.

His answer was a wordless upward jerk of the chin and a pout.

Atti said, "We must continue, before we get cold."

The four of us trudged up, stopping every hour to rest, nibble a few biscuits, and take a few gulps of water. The valley bottom was a long way below us now. We continued to climb steeply, but still couldn't make out the top. The trees merged from normal-looking oak into a weird kind of sparse forest. The trees had smooth spindly trunks, which didn't seem to know which way they should grow. They kind of writhed around, but each wore superb white flowers. James said, "Hey, those look like that old tree we climb in Granny and Granddad's garden in Six Mile Bottom. But there are lots of them here.."

Atti gave them a Nepali name and said something about foreigners visiting and taking Himalayan plants away to English gardens.

"Magnolias! That's what Granny calls them!"

"Yeah?" James responded absently, not listening, as usual.

The magnolia forest merged into pine. We were into proper snow, and still climbing. Wind tugged at my hair. The effort kept us warm in this cold, desolate place. How much further before we gained the crest of the ridge?

On and on we plodded, up and further up. Then I registered a deep, distant rumble. I saw a tiny figure far away, waving frantically at us. Was he trying to signal something? Maybe it was about whatever was causing the rumbling. Atti and Ramdin looked puzzled, too. The rumbling grew louder. Whateveritwas was coming towards us—fast.

The figure disappeared, and then I saw a massive wall of white powering down at us. There was nowhere to shelter. Atti shouted, "Run! This way. Come. Quick!"

She sprinted off at a pace I wouldn't have believed possible. We pelted after her, towards a few low-growing trees in a bit of a gully off to the side. Ramdin followed, but slowly. We ran, but this thing was fast and furious, moving at extreme speed. We weren't going to make it to the gully. I put on one last desperate spurt. It was no use.

There was a deafening roar. It hit like a train. It was shockingly cold. It sucked the air out of me. My mouth was open, but I couldn't breathe. Things hit me. I choked as snow filled my mouth. Huge forces tore at me. I was flying, tumbling. It seemed icicles were stabbing right inside me. Over and over I flew. I plunged into darkness.

"It must be dusk—when bats wake up"

13
GOING BLIND

I woke. I couldn't remember going to bed. I wasn't in bed. I opened my eyes. I couldn't see anything. I blinked. It made no difference. I rubbed my eyes. Nothing. I had gone blind. I couldn't be! Was this some awful dream? What had happened? There was a noise like water rushing. Could I hear the sea? The sound was constant. There were no waves. It was inside my head. Outside, everything was strangely quiet. Silent people were holding me down. No, not people—I was tied up. No. Something was pressing on me. I pulled an arm free. That movement was painful. It wasn't a dream.

I moved the other arm. It hurt too. I was very, very cold. It was snow that had been holding me down. I began to remember what had happened. An avalanche had hit us. I moved a bit more, and although I hurt all over, nothing seemed broken.

I got up. I was sure I was bruised everywhere. My clothes were crunchy from the frozen sweat and the snow. I dusted it off. Was it my eyes that weren't working or was it dark? But why would it be dark? It must be night time—it was pitch black. Where was I? Where was James?

I shouted. There was an echo. I wasn't outside, but how could I *not* be outside? "James! Can you hear me?" There was a muffled grunt close by. "Hey! Where are you?"

"I dunno. Can't see." His voice sounded like he was down a hole.

"Atti?" I shouted.

No answer.

"Ramdin-*dai*?"

No answer.

"Come towards my voice, Alex. Help me out, will you?"

I could hear him struggling. I got down on my hands and knees and groped towards him. The snow was so cold. "Keep talking, will you—so I can find you."

I moved forward again. My hands knocked against a strange hard object, then another, and another. They felt mostly long and thin. One was smooth, rounded on one side, but on the other there were two depressions and several sharp places. My fingers were in two eye sockets. I shuddered, throwing the revolting object from me. I'd had a human skull in my hands. Someone had died here. *We* were going to die here.

"Alex? What happened? What's up? Alex!"

"Sorry." My voice was high-pitched. I tried to make it sound normal. "I'm still here. Must be quite close now."

Then from James, "Ouch. You're on my leg!"

"Sorry. Can't see." Even this clumsy contact was a comfort.

Slowly I began to make out shapes in the gloom.

"My head hurts. I hurt—all over," James sniffed. He was trying not to cry.

110

"Yeah, I feel beaten up, too." I crawled closer and put an arm round him. "Okay?"

"Yeah. Thanks."

"We must have been unconscious for quite a while."

"Yeah. Weird, eh?"

"Yeah."

High above us, the darkness was less intense and there were smudges of light. I blinked hard and saw these were stars. I began to make out something of where we were, too. There was a slight reflection off the skull. I shivered again.

"We've fallen into some kind of pit. But I think Atti escaped. I think she got to the safety of that gulley. She might get help for us." Then my mind conjured up a picture of her. I imagined she'd reached the shelter of the low trees, but had been buried deep beneath the avalanche. No one would know. No one was around to dig her out. I felt ill. I wanted to fill the awful silence and asked, "You hungry, James?"

"Nah, just tired."

"Let's sleep a bit until morning."

"Okay—I'd like to, but it is so cold. Let's get away from the snow." We crawled around and my hands found more bones and, horrified, I realised that these animals—as well as at least one person—had fallen into the pit and never got out. I didn't tell James. We blundered around some more until we found a patch of dryish sand, snuggled together and, headachy and shivering, we fell into fitful sleep. Deep Voice's pock-marked face kept coming out of the shadows at me. "Leave me alone. You've got the ransom money."

"What?"

"Nothing—get some sleep, James."

I was still shivering when I woke. I opened and closed my hands to get some blood flowing. My left hand felt sticky. Congealed blood was the cause of the stickiness. My blood. James was stirring. A thin shaft of daylight streamed in from way above us.

"How are we going to get out of here?" I mumbled, mostly to myself. We were at the bottom of a deep hole. The avalanche had tumbled us down into a cave along with a huge pile of snow and branches and rubbish from the forest.

This hole had a wide base, but a small opening five metres above us. It was the shape of a lobster pot. The overhanging walls were almost completely smooth and there were no ledges or handholds. It had been easy to fall in, but it would be impossible to climb out. We were caught, like a couple of lobsters.

I tried scrambling up on the snow pile, but I only managed to get a couple of metres off the floor of the pit. None of the branches that had fallen inside were big enough to help either. I wandered about, walking all around the cone of debris in the middle. "Feel that, James?"

"What?"

"That warm draught..." A largish tunnel led off the lobster-pot-chamber in which we were trapped, and the draught came from it. "Surely that must mean that it leads somewhere—it'll probably connect to another entrance further down the mountain. Let's see if we can find a way out down there."

"What in there? *Into* the dark?"

"Got a better idea?"

"I dunno, but going AWAY from daylight doesn't seem too bright either..." Then his eyes lit upon the human skull and all the animal bones. He went very quiet.

"I've got a flashlight in my pocket..." I offered.

"Well, that won't last long, will it?"

"We've got matches..." I said. "We can light some of the sticks and straw and branches and stuff. We can make a kind of flaming Olympic torch!"

We gathered together some bits and pieces that might burn. I tried to avoid looking at the skull, but somehow I wanted to keep checking that it was still there. It's like when you have a sore in your mouth or tooth ache—your tongue keeps going back to check it still hurts.

I made a rough torch, but it soon felt to pieces. It was hard to keep anything alight for long. We headed into the tunnel, hoping the flashlight would last. A small frightened bat fluttered past us. The cave rapidly closed down into a passage that was so low we had to crawl. The floor was damp clay, though, so it was nice and soft for our knees. The draught through the cave was still strong, so we were confident we'd come out soon. The tunnel eventually opened up again so that we could stand.

James said, "Look Alex, point the flashlight this way, will you?"

I shone the light around and saw that we were in a chamber with a huge stalagmite column at its centre. People had been here. The stalagmite was smeared with red powder and a few coins had been left as offerings to Shiva, the god of destruction and renewal.

"This is good news, James. If people bring offerings here, there must be an easier way into this part of the cave. All we need to do is look for footprints or signs of where people have been."

"Here, Alex, there are some pieces of glass bangle. Women come in too. There must be a REALLY easy way in!"

"That's sexist!" I said.

"What's wrong with that? Boys ARE better than girls—fact. And anyway you can't do caving in a sari."

"But Nepali women do. They say that it gives them merit."

"Then they're silly." James said. "Girls are."

Forging on, we had to move in a crouching position because the cave-corridor had narrowed down again. The smell became nastier, and when the roof came down even lower and we had to stoop down and crawl, James said, "What's this stuff on the floor? It's nice and warm…. But… it's moving. What *is* it?"

"Bat guano."

"Stop calling me names, Alex!"

"I'm not. This is a huge seething pile of bat poop. That's why it smells bad."

"Why is it moving?" he asked, seeming spooked now.

"Insects. It's alive with them: feasting."

"Disgusting!"

"Don't be such a wimp. It's only woodlice and millepedes and bits of beetles. Look how they sparkle in the light."

"Ooh, lovely," he said.

Then I dropped the flashlight. It went out.

"Hey, turn the light on, Alex. I've reached a dead end."

Why did he say Dead End? That had to be pushing our luck. I groped around, my fingers moving over the sticky mud floor.

"Okay!" I shouted, "Got it!"

I switched the flashlight on. Nothing. Off and on again. Still nothing. Complete darkness. I felt for matches in my backpack. My hands were muddy, covered in thick sticky clay; I couldn't even light a match. I tried one. Two. Three. Nothing.

Finally one lit for long enough to see that we were in a small blind-ending chamber. The draught that we'd been following was streaming though a tiny slot in the rock. It was big enough for a bat, but we couldn't go on.

"Crap."

"This isn't the way then, Alex."

"No."

This wasn't the way people came into the cave to worship. We needed to go back, but I wasn't sure we'd be able to find the way back. There were no signs that people visited this part of the cave either. What now? My stomach hit my feet again. I had to sound cheerful so James wouldn't get scared.

"Okay. Let's go back the way we came for a bit. Then we'll find a side passage that'll get us out. We'll get back to the part of the cave that people visit soon."

I put my hands out like a blind man and took a step, suddenly imagining huge holes in the floor of the cave that I might fall into. Before I took the next step, I felt for solid floor with my foot. James seemed to be moving faster. I hurried to catch up with him. I walked into him and trod on his foot.

"Oi!" he shouted. "Watch it!" Then, "Ah—you can't watch it, can you!"

It was surprisingly difficult just walking along in the darkness. We felt our way, but kept crashing into each other and the cave walls. I quickly became confused about which direction we were going. I thought that I had a picture in my head of the shape of the cave we'd already come through, but I became more and more muddled. This was hopeless!

I sat down. I felt utterly miserable.

"What's happened Alex? You've stopped."

"Just having a rest," I lied.

"Time for breakfast, then!" James announced. I heard him rummaging in his backpack.

The biscuit-snack cheered me a bit, and it fired James with new enthusiasm. I heard him set off again. He often hit his head and cursed. His tuneless whistling told me that he was making good progress, though.

Then there was a scuffling and a sliding noise and a yelp and a thud.

Silence.

"James?"

Silence.

"James? Are you all right?"

Silence.

"JAMES!"

"Okay. Keep your hair on. This is a bit ticklish down here," he said. "I think I'm on a ledge. I'm going to knock a stone down." There was a short pause. I could hear him shuffling about. There was a sound of a stone bouncing off the cave walls way below me.

"Ah. It's a long way down." His voice cracked a bit. Maybe he wasn't the complete idiot I thought he was. He was scared.

That was probably good. He might not take so many risks. He was quiet for a while.

"Okay, James. I'm gonna get you out of there."

"Yeah? Try and get a match lit, Alex. I need to see how to climb out, and I don't fancy doing it in Braille."

"Okay. Wait a minute." I rubbed some of the mud off my hands. "What position are you in?"

"What do you mean, what position am I in? Down this bloody hole!"

"Yeah, but are you sitting?"

"Yeah. I'm sitting."

"Can you stand up? Then you'll get a good look even if the match only sends out a few sparks?"

"Yeah. Okay."

"Ready?"

"Yup. I'm standing."

After a few tries, I got a match lit. James was on a big ledge three metres below me and landing on that ledge had stopped him from plummeting into a deep pit. I couldn't see the bottom.

He looked down, too, and swore.

"Okay! The climb up is easy, James." I didn't need to tell him that if he made a mistake he'd fall and kill himself. "James?"

"Yeah?"

"There is a bit of a drop behind you."

"Oh, there's a bit of a drop, is there? I hadn't seen it! Wouldn't have known if you hadn't have mentioned it," he said through gritted teeth.

"Sorry. Okay. You'll be okay. It's easy. There are plenty of ledges and hand-holds. Up you come."

The match had gone out, but he'd already started to climb. I heard the sound of his breathing come closer.

"Speak!" he shouted between breaths.

"Sorry. Yeah. Okay. Sounds as if you're nearly there. I'm feeling around with my hands. Keep coming. Still okay? Like me to sing a song?"

"Only if you *want* me to fall off!"

"You must be within reach now—gotcha! Well done!" And I pulled him up beside me.

"Wow..." he said, "That was well... wow... just think what Mum'll say when I tell her! I just slipped right down. Could've gone splat at the bottom. That ledge. How lucky was that! Could've gone over the edge."

I wasn't sure what to say—even if I could have got a word in. We sat for a while in silence. Then suddenly I knew I had to make a big effort to get out of this place.

"C'mon!" I commanded. "We need to crawl more slowly now."

"Really, Alex. Why's that then?"

I didn't need his sarcasm.

We made quite good progress. We didn't speak for a while, but knew we were close by the noises of our breathing, gasping and dragging ourselves through these low passages. Then, strangely, the direction of the breeze changed, and by feeling around I realised we'd come to a junction.

"What now? Which way, James?"

"I dunno."

By now I'd completely given up trying to navigate. I wasn't even sure which direction we'd just come in. Why hadn't we got back to the seething pile of bat guano? Or the huge chamber with the stalagmite in it? Or to anywhere that we'd been before?

If we ever managed to get out of the cave now, it would be by sheer luck.

"Why hadn't we got back to the huge chamber with the stalagmite in it?"

14
DAYLIGHT

"I'm going to strike a match, James."

"Okay, but how many are left?"

"Enough," I said lying. "Okay. Ready? Ready to get a really good look at where we are?"

The match flared. We were at a point where four good-sized tunnels met.

"Which way shall we go then, James?"

"Left," he announced as he headed off down the tunnel to the right.

"Ah—the other left."

The match died. We moved on, but the image I'd seen as the match flared wouldn't change. I couldn't make my brain imagine progressing through the cave. It was so weird. It was like we were stuck in the place where we'd last been able to see. I crashed and felt and crawled, slowly moving through the cave while feeling more and more gloomy about ever finding a way out. Then I noticed that the smell of the cave had changed again—this time to a pleasant earthy smell. It felt colder too. The draught increased. Hope surged through me again.

"Let's follow the cold draught now!"

On we lumbered. I could hear James grumbling behind me. We continued until the roof became lower and lower. We were squirming on our bellies, and still the passage became smaller.

"Hey, James! I see daylight!" There was definitely a grey smudge of light up ahead. "It must be morning."

We were so close to getting out, but I could feel the cave roof scraping against my back. Then the roof became so low that there wasn't enough room to allow me to turn my head. I was squeezing between the mud floor and solid rock.

"Come on—keep going, Alex." I heard James behind me, but I couldn't go any further.

"I need to back up a bit and try further over to my left." I grunted. "It's difficult."

"Let me go first then; I'm smaller. I need to lead now."

"No, just shut up and be patient, will you." Now I was firmly wedged. I couldn't move any further forward. I felt like crying. "Back up!" I shouted at James, my voice breaking with fear and bitter disappointment.

"What do you mean, back up?"

"Go back! I can't get through. It's too small." There was daylight up ahead, but there was no way we'd ever get to it. "Back up. We'll have to try somewhere else."

I started to try to squirm in reverse, but my clothes kept snagging on the cave roof. I couldn't find the point in this passage where I could go back. I couldn't turn around either. I was so scared.

"It's okay," I talked to myself. "I can do this. A little at a time." I knew that the more fearful I became, the more tense I'd get, which would make it more difficult to move. I didn't want to die in this awful tight muddy place. Then I totally lost it. I thrashed around with my feet. That achieved nothing.

"Talk to me, James. I can't work out how to get back."

His reply came from over to the left, and I wriggled towards him. I got to another place which was too small for me. "I'm stuck again," I said in a shaky voice. "My top ear is scraping on the roof and my bottom ear is squeezed into the mud. I don't like this." I felt the cave roof with my feet. I then reversed into solid rock. "I can't do this!"

"Try over to the right—it feels bigger over there."

"Which way is right?" I asked.

"Umm..." A few moments later I felt him pulling my ankle. "It's better from here, I think, Alex."

It was a bit higher on the right. I wriggled over that way.

"Great. Fantastic. Wonderful. Brilliant. Thanks."

Suddenly I was all right again. I'd stopped thrashing around wildly. I was making slow steady progress, but how I longed to get into a passage that was high enough to allow us to get up on our knees again. I kept squirming backwards, being stopped often by solid rock or James' head. Finally, though, we were into a passage that was big enough for us to sit up again.

"Glad I'm out of there. I didn't enjoy that at all."

"I guessed. So... what now? Shall I try?"

"No, James—I don't think it's worth it... You won't fit through either."

"What else can we do?" he asked, putting the dampers on my relief.

"We'd better go back the way we came, again. We'll feel along the walls on either side as we go, and if we don't find any new passages, we'll have to try to find that cross-roads." So back we went. Our heads were getting more and more sore—from bashing into lumps sticking out of the cave roof. Then there was more cursing from James. "Poop. Pustules. Puke. I can't find a way on. This is another dead end."

"Look, stop saying 'Dead End!' It's spooky. I want to sit down for a bit. Let's rest. I've had it." And so we sat on the sticky-mud floor of the blind-ending chamber and once again I heard James rummaging for biscuits. We leant against each other for comfort and warmth. Once the last of the biscuits was eaten, we became silent for a while. "You all right?"

"Yeah."

"Any ideas?"

"Nah."

My mind was racing. Surely we'd go mad, just sitting here in the dark. I asked, "Know any jokes?"

"Jokes? Yeah, okay, what's brown and sounds like a bell?"

"Dunno," I said. "Look actually I'm not in the mood for your stupid riddles, James."

"Come on—try."

"I really don't know."

"Shall I tell you then?"

"Okay," I said.

"Dung."

"How does dung sound like a bell?"

"You know—dung... ding dong.... Dung? It's a very dunny

joke. Get it? Dung in a dunny?" he said. "That's Australian for toilet, you know!"

"Your spur-of-the-moment jokes are even worse that the old ones you torture us with," I said. "And it's not a very good joke if you have to explain it."

"It's not my fault if you're too thick to get my jokes, Alex!"

"Let's..."

"Yeah, let's try again. I've got another," James said. "What is brown and sticky?"

"Dung. What is it with you and poop?"

"No. Dung's not the answer. Try again," he said triumphantly.

"Poop."

"No—like I just said—it's nothing to do with poop. Think of something else that's brown and sticky."

"I dunno.... Toffee?"

"No, wrong. A stick!"

"You are such an idiot, James."

Next he suggested, "Let's play consequences."

"I'm really not in the mood," I said.

"I'll start.... Rocks."

"Bones..." I said, sighing.

"Muscles."

"Skeleton."

"Body."

"Coffin... no look: this is giving me the creeps," I said.

"Let's sing a song instead."

"No. I hate singing," I replied.

"How about I-spy?"

"That's a really stupid idea, James."

"No, it's not. I spy with my little eye something beginning with N," he chanted.

"Dunno."

"Do you give up?"

"Yeah."

"Do you really? Don't you want a clue?"

"No."

"Shall I tell you then?"

"Yeah."

"Nothing!"

"What?"

"Nothing—that's the answer."

"Woo-hoo."

"I have another one." He wouldn't be stopped. "I spy with my little eye something beginning with D."

"Dunno."

"Ha-ha. Yeah, that begins with D, but it isn't that. Go on— guess again."

"Don't know."

"Do you give up?"

"Yeah."

"Dark. I've thought of another one. I spy with my little eye something beginning with B."

"This is really stupid. I don't know."

"Why don't you try to guess?"

"I'm *really, really* not in the mood."

"Do you give up, then?"

"Yeah."

"Black. Three out of three. I win!"

"Yeah, yeah, okay. You won," I said.

We sat in silence for a while, then James asked, "Do you believe in ghosts?"

"Not really," I said, wondering whether I did or not.

"That woman in the last tea shop did, didn't she?"

"Yeah; lots of Nepalis believe in things like that."

"Do you think there are ghosts in here?" James asked.

Just the thought made the hairs at the back of my neck stand on end.

There were no sounds except our breathing, and the occasional drip, drip of water. The darkness was awesome and immense. It was so strange to be able to see nothing at all. It was so completely black that I imagined shapes and distant sparks, but there were none.

"Well?" James said.

"Well what?"

"Do you think there are ghosts?"

"No." But really—at that moment—I knew there probably were.

"Remember that skull we found, Alex?"

"Yeah."

"I bet his ghost is in here."

"Shut up, James."

The water *drip-dripped*. In the distance I was sure I could hear someone else breathing. Perhaps it was a dream. We must have drifted off to sleep.

Later—it may have been seconds, minutes or hours—I was awake again, feeling chilled, cold, and desolate. All I could hear was James' deep steady breathing and the slow drip, dripping.

After a while, there was another sound...in the distance.

I strained to hear. Nothing. But then, there it was again. It was a kind of fluttering. Then it stopped again. I'd probably imagined it. James was right. There were ghosts: the ghosts of people who had died in this cave.

How I wished James would wake up.

A few minutes later I was sure that there was a fluttering sound again. It was a bit like a bird flapping to get through a closed window. The sound grew louder and came closer, then a *tick-ticking* came with the noise. The air moved as something ghostly fluttered past me. A bat flew along our cave-corridor. Another came and another: loads of them.

It must be dusk—when bats wake up. Or maybe it was dawn, when they come home to sleep. I had no idea how long we'd been underground. Could we really have been underground all day and half the night?

I thought of following the bats, but were they flying deeper into the cave or towards an entrance, or even back to that lobster-pot hole that we'd fallen into? Or were they flying towards that impassable passage that we'd already tried and failed to get through? Or was there yet another entrance? We had to find out. That gave me an idea. Maybe I could sense the way out from the echo.

I shouted. The walls sounded close. I tried shouting high and low. James stirred, but didn't wake. The lower sounds seemed to echo better. It seemed as if there was an echo coming back from further away.

"Come on, James. Let's move."

He grumbled, but woke up. I got stiffly onto my knees again and started to crawl forward, towards the more distant echo, until my head hit rock.

"Ow!" I shouted; the echo was completely different. I crawled a bit further, again toward where it sounded furthest. My head hit rock again, and I cursed. "How do bats do this?"

"What are you on about? I told you it was a dead end," James said sleepily. "Why bother?"

The woman in the last tea shop had said that people sometimes visit the cave to worship on Saturdays. Maybe when they came they would find us. We'd entered on Thursday. How long had we been inside? Maybe Saturday had come and gone, and we'd have to wait another week to be rescued. Or maybe this was a labyrinth of tunnels, and visitors only entered a small part of a huge and complex cave system. Maybe there were miles and miles and miles of passages.

We might never see our parents again, and they'd never know what had happened to us. How sad they would be.... I crawled back to James, who had stopped moving, snuggled up and drifted off to sleep again, dreaming of sunbathing on the beach, nibbling chocolate. It was a brilliant dream, until something cold and slimy crawled out of the sea....

When I woke up again, I was shivering violently. I was chilled to the centre of my bones. I shook myself. I tried to shrug away the cold. It was as if that slimy sea-creature had crept right inside me, though I knew it hadn't. I was stiff and still sore. James had keeled over and was sleeping soundly on his side close to me. He was breathing easily, seemingly without a care in the world. We had to try to find a way out. What was the point though? A voice inside my head told me I should stir myself. I must at least try, but I didn't feel like it. I didn't care any more. I wished I could sleep.

A few cat-naps later, I thought I heard something different.

I strained again to hear. It was just water dripping...or bats. I heard the noise again. It wasn't bats this time. I concentrated so hard that it almost hurt. I shook James awake. "Can you hear anything? I thought I was dreaming, but I think there is something... listen."

"*Urgh?*"

"Can you hear anything?"

"No..... yeah. Is it water? Is the cave flooding?" This was a new and dreadful possibility. I'd heard of caves filling up and people getting trapped for weeks. Or divers going in to rescue them. No one would come for us. We'd starve—or drown.

I listened again. It was nothing. Was I going mad? Was I imagining things?

"No, surely, that's people talking and laughing, isn't it?"

"It can't be!" James said miserably. Then, "Yeah it is. No it isn't. Oh, I dunno."

"Let's shout!" I said. "Together. One, Two, Three, HELP!"

There were shrieks and giggles in reply. We shouted again, "Hey! People!"

Several voices replied from within the cave.

Grey patches appeared and disappeared. There was a lightening of the cave roof. Shapes we could hardly see flickered and moved inside our eyes. Strange ghostly shadows darted around the small chamber we were sitting in. Bumps in the rock wall threw odd dancing shadows. The voices grew clearer. They were children's voices, shouting with excitement from somewhere above us. There was light at last. It moved around, highlighting different parts of the small chamber that I thought would become our tomb.

It was smaller than the smallest bedroom imaginable,

130

and the ceiling was so low that I couldn't stand upright in it. The walls looked beautifully carved and smoothed, by water I suppose; now I saw that the roughness in the cave walls that had snagged my clothes was fossil sea-shells. The flickering light grew brighter, and the voices grew louder.

Then I saw a candle sticking out from the middle of a fist that was completely encased in wax. The wax fist was shoved through a small hole in the ceiling. A head followed with a huge grin.

"What are you doing there, brothers!"

"We're lost... we are SO happy to see you. We thought we'd never find our way out!"

"You speak truly. This is a most dangerous place. Come! This way. Climb up here."

He grabbed my arm and pulled me up through the slender opening to sit beside him. He was about my age, but much more muscled. The dancing candle-flame made his face look ghostly, and I suddenly wondered whether this was another weird dream—until he slapped me on the back. Then he reached down for James. We three sat grinning at each other for a while, until a girl's shrill voice asked what was going on. She wanted to see the strangers, too.

Then all eight rescuers squeezed forward at once. They were so keen to see us, they got jammed between the cave walls. The oldest boy told them to be patient. The arguing and pushing continued. Each of them wanted to be the one to guide us out. Each one of them seemed to have a different story about people who had visited the cave. They talked—all at once—about all the people who had been rescued.

Then one boy said, "I will tell you one more thing. There

is bad air in some parts of the cave also. You were most fortunate not to have entered those places where there is no oxygen. These are very terrible places, but they are far from here. There is no need to worry."

I did worry though. How horrible was the thought of suffocating in the dark? But then I suppose it would be quick. Better than slowly starving.

The children led us back to the big chamber. They stopped at the huge stalagmite. The oldest boy pulled a few grains of rice from his pocket and placed them in front of the red-daubed column. Tiny glistening white springtails ran in to feast on the offerings.

While the children were saying a few quick prayers, I said to James, "It is unbelievable getting back here so quickly. I thought that we were hours away from this place!"

"Yeah."

One of our rescuers said, "We are giving thanks to Shiva for sending us to find you. We don't usually come into the cave on this day. Maybe Lord Shiva put the idea into our heads. You also must salute him." We put the palms of our hands together and quickly nodded our thanks. I looked around wondering if they expected us to do more than that, but they were already walking on—leading us to freedom.

"Tiny glistening white springtails ran in to feast on the offerings"

15
GOOD SMELLS

We walked along with our excited rescuers. I was stumbling with exhaustion at first, but then realised how easy it was now simply putting one foot in front of the other. It was wonderful to see again, and then we were blinded by the sunlight. It stabbed at our eyes, making them water. Slowly, we blinked away tears and saw colour again. A gentle breeze moved my hair.

The fresh air was so full of good smells—of mouldering leaves, of dust, of perfume from the shrubs. The children laughed at the way we stood just looking and breathing. How easily we could have died in the still, sterile blackness. How easily we were rescued. They ordered us to come to their village to eat and rest and recover. Their bossy kindness was just what we needed.

As soon as we arrived in the village, women and girls came and fussed around us. They brought brass teapots of water and poured for us so we could wash some of the bat poop and cave clay off our hands. Gigglingly, they pouted at our faces, ordering us to wash there, too. They thrust roasted sweet corn into our hands. It smelt deliciously nutty. It wasn't until we started to eat that we realised how incredibly hungry we were.

They gave us cloth *lungis** to wrap around us like bath towels and, ignoring our protests, took away our ripped trousers. As my eyes tracked the young girl who marched off with our clothes, I noticed a small man in combats sitting on a verandah*. I grabbed James' arm and jerked my chin towards the man. I felt James tense. A girl from the house looked at the direction of our gaze, then whistled to attract the man's attention. But it was an unknown face, and we sighed in relief.

The evening rice and curry was the best ever. Once we'd eaten, I said, "It's so good to be free. We are so lucky you found us."

"It is not luck. It is your good *karma*," a teenage boy said.

"Have you seen any other strangers, *dai*?" I asked. "A Nepali girl was with us."

The villagers discussed who had been seen, and the boy replied, "No girl-strangers..."

I was just starting to wonder what had happened to our clothes when two girls returned them to us beautifully sewn and patched. Hills people are so generous with what little they have. I felt bad about having nothing with which to repay their kindness. We settled down to sleep on their verandah, savouring the smells of wood-smoke and cow dung and even of unwashed people.

The following day I woke slowly. I was in a soft warm bed between clean sheets, and I could smell bacon frying in the kitchen.

Something wasn't right though. The smell was changing, and there was a whiff of bat guano in my nostrils. The pillow under my head was lumpy and hard. I could feel the seeds that were mixed in with the stuffing from silk-cotton pods; they must have made pock-marks in my face. That thought brought Deep Voice's face back into my head. Small creatures were skittering around on my skin. I had bites all over, and each little bump on my skin itched horribly.

I was properly awake now. I wasn't in a bed, but lying on a rice-straw mat under a grubby but deliciously soft cotton-stuffed quilt on the verandah of our rescuers. My breath formed steamy clouds in the cold, cold air. I was aching from all that crawling around in the cave. My knees and elbows and the palms of my hands were scratched and sore.

I snuggled up, hoping to return to my cosy dream, but the fleas were biting me again and soon drove me to get up. James was a heap at the other end of the verandah, and his deep breathing told me he was still fast asleep. I sauntered around the back of the little house and found the long-drop* toilet. It was an outhouse built of stone and perched on the edge of a steep bank. I *could* do a strip wash in there, but there was no water. I stood peering into the unattractive cubicle, deliberating, when James, suddenly awake, pushed past me and went inside.

As he opened the creaky door of the long-drop to leave, I thought of shoving him back inside to see if he'd fall down the hole, but my bladder wouldn't let me mess about. And once I was inside with my bladder empty, I saw that wouldn't have worked anyway; the hole was too small. A bitingly cold wind blew up through it. There was earth piled up in the corner of the toilet, and a shovel. After you'd pooped, you were supposed to chuck down a spadeful to cover it. That's why there wasn't much smell, I suppose. Business done, I was outside again and turned towards a sound below me—down the bank. A man was shovelling unmentionable stuff out of the bottom of the long-drop. Dad had told me before that all the poop that falls down the hole, composts into a harmless power, which can then be used to fertilise the fields. Clever really, but I wasn't sure I'd want his job.

Apropos poop, I almost envied my little brother for his straight hair that poop falls out of so easily. My curls seemed to cling onto the bat droppings, but even so I decided against washing. I'd stay smelly a bit longer. Back on the verandah, people were gathering round again to ask us more questions. No one had seen Atti. I just hoped she was safe. I felt so guilty about not being able to search for her, but what could we do? I didn't even know where the avalanche had hit us, and the children didn't seem to know about it. Someone *had* seen a Nepali man walking alone, but they'd hidden and hadn't got a good look at him.

I tried to steer the conversation back to what we needed to know. I wanted to get an idea of what these people thought about Maoists. They all had very strong views. They told us of all the threats that the Maoists made, and how these villagers had been forced to contribute food and money for a cause that they didn't support—not any more. We decided to take a risk and explained about our parents.

136

"Ah. My sister said that she had seen two foreigners, a man and a woman. The woman was limping, and they were going slowly. If you boys walk down off the ridge by this path—this way," our teenage friend pouted with his lips towards a river way, way below us, "I think that you will have a chance of catching up, but then what will you do? You alone cannot rescue your parents from these powerful, ruthless men—with guns... Do you have guns?"

"No. We don't know what we'll do," I said miserably, "but we must try..."

"Before you go," he said, "we must do a special *puja**. Let us return to the cave and give offerings to Shiva so that he will speed your journey and destroy your enemies."

I knew we needed all the help we could get and I didn't want to offend our new friends, but there was NO WAY that I was going back into that cave. They laughed at our fearfulness, but I think they understood. We made our excuses and left.

A couple of hours walking down lonely broken paths took us to the river again. The exercise and the sun warmed us nicely.

"Hey, James?"

"Yeah?"

"Let's stop and wash."

"What's wrong with you?" he asked frowning. "You don't *like* washing!"

"These fleas are driving me mad." I stripped naked, laid out my clothes in the sun, and watched the fleas hop away looking for somewhere to hide from the light. James stared for a bit. "Looks like your leg's healing."

"Yeah."

He started scratching again and said, "Worth a try I suppose." He stripped too.

The river was icy, so we decided against bathing, just rinsing our hands and forearms and splashing a bit of water on our faces. It stung our wounds, but it made us feel a bit better. It also got rid of some of the cave smell. Getting dressed again, though, we realised how amazingly rank our clothes were. Mine were just as smelly as James' now; his rhino poop perfume had been overwhelmed long ago. We didn't care. We just plodded wearily on along the river.

"This is hopeless," James said.

"What is?"

"How ever will we find Mum and Dad now?"

"We've gotta try." The path was stony and uneven, so we had to watch where we placed each step. "There's a very good chance they came this way."

Then unexpectedly, we were met by the cheering sight of a tea shop and the prospect of a hot drink. "This is *really* good news! Someone might have seen Mum and Dad! Or there might be news of Atti."

"Let's hope."

"Hey! Look!" I grabbed James' arm to stop him. He protested, not wanting anything to get between him and sweet tea and biscuits.

"What?" he said, pulling away irritably.

"Look, will you!" I pointed. Was so excited I could hardly get the words out. "Aren't those Mum's?"

"What are you talking about?"

He looked and saw that outside the flimsy-looking shack, in the place where porters leave their loads, was a pair of walking poles. These were distinctive, because their owner had decorated them with bands of different coloured tape. "They *are* Mum's!"

"I think you're right! Hey, you are right, Alex. Amazing!"

"We've actually found them!" Then I thought again. They could have been stolen, or sold.

"Let's get a closer look."

Someone appeared in the doorway of the tea shop. A man. I quickly saw that we were in great danger of being seen. He might have nothing to do with the kidnap, or he might be one of the gang. I dragged James off the path and into some scrub. It was a great hiding place. People had dug red mud out of it to wash with and for plastering their houses, so there was a depression to conceal ourselves in.

The man set off at a brisk pace towards us. We hunkered down low and kept still. I got a terrible itch just as the man walked past, but I managed to resist scratching. He walked on towards the lowlands. Once he was out of sight, we took another look at the tea shop.

"It's quite a big place, Alex. There could be a dozen people inside."

"Yeah. If Mum and Dad are guarded by several men, we'll never get them free."

"Let's at least have a look. They might already have escaped!"

"Huh, some hopes."

"Come on then! What are we waiting for?"

Circling around off the path, we arrived at the back of the tea shop, where we could get close to a glassless window. We could hear what was going on inside quite clearly. Deep

Voice was there, and so was Dad, talking to him—reasoning with him. Dad sounded really tired. I sneaked a peek. The two men sitting opposite my parents held ancient rifles. A third had his back to us. He looked better dressed than the others and wore a traditional Nepali hat. The fourth was the pock-marked deep-voiced little man whose face was familiar from the encounter in the jungle—and from my nightmares.

Dad looked half-starved. There were deep shadows around his eyes—and Mum's too. Mum's hair looked like a bush—complete with twigs. But it was so good to see them!

Deep Voice sounded harsh. He seemed angry with our parents. "Your boys only delivered some of the ransom money. What have they done with the other million?"

"I don't know, really I don't. They wouldn't have taken it. Maybe there was some mix up. We'll get it. I promise. Let us go, and we'll get it for you..."

Some of the money must still be up in the monkey tree, but Deep Voice thought we'd deliberately cheated him, and he was furious. "You foreigners do so much cheating. Foreigners cannot be trusted. You should get out of my country. You think you know what is best for Nepal, but you know nothing: not about our ancient culture, not about what we need, not about anything. We don't want your filthy aid money either. You people, and the Americans, are interfering too much in my country, but no more!"

"I don't know why you hate us so much," Dad mumbled. "We were really trying to help."

"Help? Help yourselves, I am thinking! Now, though, you *will* help. When news of your abduction reaches the world press, then you foreigners will stop coming. It will be better

140

for us. Actually, it will be best if you do not survive."

"No...really...there's a lot we can do together, in partnership. Truly."

I was paralysed with fear. I couldn't think straight. What were we going to do now? What could we do? We sat for a long time hidden amongst some scratchy bushes, thinking, knowing we couldn't fight these grown men with guns. Then the tea shop owner said something that made the well-dressed man turn. It was that Tek Bahadur again, the man with the fine moustache who had seemed so friendly when we'd first met him, but who had been spying on us and had tried to follow us. What *was* going on?

The tea shop owner came outside to draw some water from the hand-pump.

"Psst! Psst! Sister!" I caught her attention and beckoned her over.

"Hey son!" she said, a little surprised.

"Please talk quietly, *didi*. We are in trouble and we need your help."

"How can I help the little *sahibs*?"

"Those men inside—are they good men?"

"No, these are not good men! They are Maoists. I think that they have captured that man and that woman. They look scared. These men have weapons also."

"They are our parents!" I whispered. "Look, if I give you some money..." I pulled out a crumpled damp 500-rupee note with tigers on it. "Will you give those men lots to drink? So that they get *really* drunk?"

"I think that this will be easy." The wrinkly woman smiled showing that she had only one tooth. "I should like to do something against these people. They said they would lead a revolution to help the poor and stop us going hungry. They lied—and they have killed innocent people. My brother tried to stop one bad piece of business. They were sending young girls away to Mumbai. They threatened him—told him not to make trouble. When he refused to keep quiet, they sent their thugs in the night, with an axe. He nearly died from the beating. He lost a leg also. The police did nothing. These Maoists don't care about the poor any more than the politicians in Kathmandu. No one cares about us—except our families. We still go hungry."

She walked back inside.

"Who were you talking to, old woman?" Deep Voice asked.

"You would show some respect if you were really Maoist. And I was talking to my goats and chickens. They eat nicely if I sing to them. I am a little bit worried about one of my goats. I think she has been eating plastic bags again. It is a new problem. A few years back if you bought something in Chisapaani market, it would be put in a paper bag made out of old newspaper. My goats liked eating these. Now everyone uses plastic, and it is not good for the goats. They..."

"You have goats?" One of the kidnappers interrupted. "Then bring us meat!" he demanded.

"I have goats. You have no manners. I will bring meat soon—maybe."

"Mad old woman," Deep Voice mumbled. Then unexpectedly he got up. He stepped outside. My mouth went dry. There was no time to hide. We just kept frozen still hoping he wouldn't notice us. He stood framed in the tiny doorway of the hut. He pulled a nasty, lethal-looking *khukuri** from his

142

"He pulled a lethal-looking khukuri from his belt"

belt and started picking dirt out from under his fingernails with it. He paused for a moment and looked around. His eyes rested on my legs. His gaze travelled up over my body to my face. Then he saw James. He waved his weapon at us, indicating we should go inside. I read hatred his face.

"Look what I found!"

My parents' mouths opened, but they said nothing.

Deep Voice just said "Sit. You children are as irritating as horseflies...now my men will have to look after four hostages. This they might find quite inconvenient."

He next said something in very fast Nepali. I couldn't follow it, but Mum and Dad looked even more scared.

Then, quite abruptly, Deep Voice got up. He waggled his head saying "*Jaom*" and left with Tek Bahadur. I watched them stride off back towards Chisapaani. I was so frightened I couldn't think clearly. I looked to Mum and Dad for guidance, but they looked exhausted, defeated. I tried to reason that surely, now that there were only two guards, we might have a better chance to get free, but as if they sensed what I was thinking, one pointed his rifle at me. Much as I tried to persuade myself otherwise, our situation seemed hopeless.

"What happens now, Dad?"

"They don't want us to know..."

One Maoist snapped at Dad in Nepali, "Shut your mouth."

Dad looked at his feet.

There was a tatty picture of Ganesh pinned up behind Dad. In my head, I said to the elephant-headed god, help us out, won't you mate?

Then to my astonishment, the tea shop owner began chuckling gently to herself. She addressed the Maoists, "Have you tried this new pineapple-flavoured wine? It is good. It is a special new variety from India. It is tasty. Take some."

Her hand with its blackened, broken fingernails closed around the bottle. We watched as she poured thick, sick-yellow vodka. The kidnappers loved it. They greedily grabbed a lurid bottle each, poured it out and gulped it down. Soon they stopped bothering to use glasses, swigging it straight from the bottle.

The kidnappers grew drunker and drunker. They giggled like schoolgirls, but they also got friskier—not sleepier—with each glass. Maybe the drink wouldn't make them pass out!

Dad falls asleep after only one or two small drinks. Maybe it was different with hardened drinkers? Maybe our plan was starting to work, though. The kidnappers were getting drunker and sillier. They soon looked as if they didn't care about anything.

James started to fidget. Now that they were half drunk, I wondered if we had a chance to rush them and bash them over the head like they do in the films. It seemed far too risky.

"Where is the meat you promised? Must I go out and shoot one of your goats myself?"

"You're drunk—and rude. Go home if you don't like my

hospitality!"

Knowing that he risked getting no more vodka, the kidnapper changed the subject. Conversationally, he complained about the price and quality of rice and lentils in the market at Chisapaani. He complained about how Indians run all the stalls now and how they make big profits....

The two remaining kidnappers drank another bottle of vodka. And another, until finally their giggles faded and they slid slowly onto the floor. One fell off his bench right in the doorway. I poked the nearest Maoist and got no reaction.

The old woman said, "You must go quickly."

Mum and Dad nodded and crept passed the snoring Maoists. Our parents had to be extra quiet as they stepped over the man in the doorway. Soon we were outside, hugging.

"Come on quickly!" I said. "Let's take this dugout boat." We all started moving down to the river, with Mum limping horribly. "Hang on just a minute...." I said as I ran back up to the tea shop and spoke to the old woman again. "*Didi*, please give this money to the person who owns the boat. I don't know when we'll be able to bring it back."

She grinned—a broad gummy grin. "A thousand rupees is a good price for my son's *dinghy**. Here—take the paddles also. Go with good fortune. You are good boys."

"Until we meet again, *didi*," I said saluting her with my hands together as in prayer.

I ran back down to the beach and helped Dad push the heavy dugout canoe into the river—into the friendly river that would take us back to the Plains, and help.

Finally, we'd escaped. No one could catch us now... or so I foolishly thought.

"Asian small-clawed otters watched the family escape in a dugout made from a red silk-cotton tree"

16
PREDATORS

We'd rescued our parents, but this wobbly dugout canoe felt pretty unstable. Suddenly the river didn't feel friendly any more. The current caught the boat and spun it broadside. It rocked horribly. We all bent forwards trying to get as low as we could. I was sure we'd capsize. It swung further around. Now the dugout was pointing upstream. Dad cursed under his breath, but Mum managed to spin it around again.

I concentrated on keeping still and keeping my head low. It felt safer like that. My focus was on the inside of the boat. It had been roughly hacked out of a single tree-trunk. I pressed my nail into the wood and made a mark; this was soft, light, and easy to carve—a silk-cotton tree then.

The river fought to spin us around. Mum and Dad struggled to keep us straight. They power-paddled us downstream. Flashes of sunlight reflected off the water, dazzling me. I scanned around, checking for other tell-tale reflections. It was too easy to be seen. We'd be silhouetted against the water. Might Deep Voice or one of the others get a message to his gang so that they could capture us again? The relief I'd felt when we'd first got Mum and Dad free was evaporating fast.

"Do you know what river this is, Dad? Do you know where it'll take us?"

He scanned around, frowning. "Not sure, Alex, but we're going south. Towards the towns of the Plains, and help. We're doing a decent speed, too."

"Yeah, that's got to be good. Maybe, somehow, we'll have a chance of getting the ransom money back. Are you going to tell us what happened? How we got into this mess?"

The boat rocked violently. We all sat as low in the boat as we could and concentrated on keeping afloat. I kept gingerly looking over my shoulder, expecting trouble. I couldn't stop thinking that somehow the kidnappers would catch up with us. They probably had a network. Maybe messages were going out about us now. I felt better though as we travelled further and further away. The sun warmed me. I told myself that things were going to be okay.

The deep foamy water slopped against the boat. There was a whistle from close by. Mum jumped slightly. Dad looked alarmed, then scanned around to see who was communicating with whom.

"What's going on?" I asked no one in particular.

There was another noise, like someone breathing out sharply—almost a sneeze. I found myself staring into big round predatory eyes. The cruel kidnappers' faces came back to me for a moment. My mind was playing tricks. I was looking at a predator all right, but this was an otter. Two more otter heads popped out of the water to examine us, then three

148

more. One whistled, another replied, and they all dived. A few seconds later they surfaced again on the other side of the boat. They kept with us for several hundred metres.

Mum said, "Look how they touch noses to keep contact with each other." She reached over and gave me a squeeze. "Thanks for everything, Alexander..."

I wished she wouldn't do stuff like that, but when I turned to say something, I could see she was all choked up. I kept quiet. The river widened and slowed, and one otter whistled for the others not to follow. She led them up-stream again to continue fishing. The otters disturbed a couple of hand-sized flap-shelled mud turtles that had been sunbathing on the river-bank. They plopped into the water, for safety.

"So what's the plan then, Dad?"

"Not sure, but we'll need to contact the Embassy, and the police, I suppose. I wish I knew whom we can trust, and I wish I knew which river this was."

"This looks familiar, ya know. Do you recognise it, James?"

"Not sure."

I turned around carefully, still nervous of tipping the dugout over. Behind were the mighty snow-covered Himalayas. Ahead I could see that the river was narrowing and speeding up. We were approaching a gorge. It *was* the Chisapaani Gorge—our gorge. As we shot into its shade, the canoe picked up speed, and all Mum and Dad needed to do was keep us pointing downstream. That wasn't as easy as it sounds: the boat was unstable and kept lurching and threatened to turn right over. The current caught the tail end. I heard Mum gasp. She kept looking over her shoulder, too. Eddies threatened to spin us broadside again. Mum and Dad were paddling hard and breathing hard.

The river was deep and green and narrow here. We had to crane our heads backwards to see to the top of the gorge walls. "Hey, look, there's where we fell in." James said.

"Where?" Dad asked.

"Right up there—from that little ledge."

"What? There?!" Dad cried out. Mum groaned slightly. She was unusually quiet.

I saw the sandy beach where I'd been washed up. Two big gharials were sunning themselves.

"They look mean!" James said. The strange thin crocodile snout was armed with a double line of chain-saw teeth. The gharials had already slipped off into the river.

We swept on through the gorge, under the vast Chisapaani Bridge and on down the river, which splits to flow each side of the huge island of Rajapur.

"Big gharials were sunning themselves on the sandy beach"

We took the smaller channel—to the right, to the west of the island. This would take us close to Rajapur town. Mum said, "It is good to see people again. We're safe now."

The sounds of joking and singing carried across to us.

James said, "Look—the kids are gathering bags of little *bayar* fruit....."

Dad said, "We'll get some grub soon. I could eat a whole buffalo."

"Look—see those women down at the water's edge over there?" Mum said, pointing.

I reckon she was trying to distract us: stop us thinking about all the scary stuff that had happened. I humoured her. "Yeah. So what *are* they doing?"

"Panning for gold."

"Cool—we should try." James' interest in money was only second to his interest in chocolate.

"Yes, but not now, James. You know it takes some skill—like the way Atti is so good at getting the stones out of rice by throwing it around on that tray-thing she has."

Atti. Was she okay? I'd almost convinced myself that she'd escaped. She was probably safely back with her family in Rajapur. Or so I hoped.

Meanwhile, James sat thoughtfully mining snot from his nose. There was another unexpected noise. We were all looking in different directions. The boat rocked alarmingly.

"What was that?"

"I don't know," Dad said, looking worried.

There was a splash. I turned, half expecting a boat to be bearing down on us, but what I saw instead was a greyish pink back and a big ring of ripples. "A dolphin!"

"Yes, a dolphin." Everyone was smiling, relieved. We scanned the now mill-pond-still river so that we'd see the dolphin the next time it surfaced to breathe. A full two minutes later we saw its strangely thin beak poke out of the water. We had a good enough glimpse to see the dimples where the eyes should have been, and the dorsal fin that is little more than a bump. We tapped on the side of the boat, and it came over. Then it dived. We didn't see it again.

Another movement, a shadow moving over the water, caught my attention. Why did something like that make me jumpy? It was only a black and white bird. It hovered high above us with its large beak pointed straight down. It folded its wings, plummeted into the river and flapped to the surface again with a fish in its beak. "Pied kingfisher," Dad said.

"Did you say pie?" James said. I reckon he deliberately misunderstood so as to distract Dad from giving another wildlife lecture. "I'd like some pie...."

"No, Mr. Brain-in-your-stomach," Dad said. "I was pointing out a pied kingfisher—the black and white kind."

"I don't mind any kind of pie: kingfisher, chicken, bee-eater, vulture, meat, apple, porky pie, even snake and pigmy..." James looked wistful and licked his lips.

Dad smiled. The river sped up over some pebble shoals and then calmed again. After a while, Mum said, "What *is* that black stuff on your shin Alexander?"

"Umm. I met this croc... I mean branch... in the river. A nice woman in a tea shop put battery innards on it. She called it *dawai*..."

"Hmm; it doesn't *look* like medicine."

"Yeah, but it seems to have worked because my leg has stopped throbbing. Feels much better."

Mum wrinkled her nose. I could see she was scanning around, looking for something else to talk about. She said, "When we get to Rajapur, I think we should go straight to the police. They'll be able to tell the Embassy. They'll help. Ooh, hey, look boys, an osprey! Look he's going to dive..."

I must have given her a funny look.

She continued, "Don't look so worried, Alex, we're safe now. You got us away. The adventure is over, thanks to you."

"And me!" James added.

"Yes, and you, James."

Finally, after another hour or so we pulled the canoe onto a familiar silty beach, close to the house we used to rent. Mum was limping badly as we set off up the beach. I asked her, "Are you okay? What happened to your leg?"

"Oh, it's nothing much," she said. "I twisted my knee again, coming down a long descent. Annoying really, but its nothing that a bit of rest and some food won't fix. Come on—let's get to the police station and get things sorted out."

We sauntered towards the centre of the bazaar. The smell of women cooking their evening curry made my mouth water. Dusk was gathering. A waist-deep wake of dust hung over the road, churned up by a passing buffalo cart. Someone up ahead seemed to have lost his legs and the rest of him was cruising ghost-like above the miasma; as he walked on, the dust ate him up completely. Then a misty flotilla of cyclists loomed towards us. At first all that was visible of the bicycles were the handlebars; the men's knees popped up alternately out of the weird soup as they worked the pedals.

James had his thoughts elsewhere, "Can we buy a samosa, please?"

"A samosa? Terrible idea. We need several—each," Dad said, and we stopped to watch the stall-holder carefully place twelve into a paper bag made out of someone's English homework. We scoffed them in seconds and continued our stroll through the bazaar towards the police station, our mouths tingling deliciously from the chillies.

"A house gecko above us uttered his odd grinding call"

17
THE CHIEF INSPECTOR OF POLICE

Arjun stood under the ceiling fan behind a huge battered desk. The police station was gloomy, but he grinned broadly as he recognised us. His children, Siru, Biru and of course little Atti, were our playmates when we'd lived in Rajapur a year or two before. Our families were close. But his brow folded into furrows as he saw the state we were in. "Good to see you—but what happened?"

Atti *hadn't* told him anything.

Then I thought some more and my guts contracted. The last time we saw her was moments before that avalanche hit and fired us into the cave. I suddenly felt sick. Perhaps she hadn't got back. Perhaps it had hit her too. Perhaps she was still buried under a pile of snow. I was going to say something, but knew my voice wouldn't sound normal. I swallowed hard.

I was relieved when Dad spoke, "It's a long story, Arjun-*dai*." He said wearily. "Could we see the Chief Inspector please? He's a new man, isn't he?"

"Yes, a new man, with new ways." Arjun's tone told us that

he didn't like his new boss. "It is big trouble then if you need to see Inspector-*sahib*. Look, I'll send the boy to the hotel for some food for you. OK?"

"That would be wonderful!" the four of us said together. The samosas we'd eaten had reminded us how very hungry we were.

Soon a scrawny child brought four glasses of sweet steaming tea. I heard Mum mumbling to herself, "Twice James' age and half his size." The kid scuttled out to bring our food. We sat to await an audience with the officer in charge.

I asked Arjun, "How is Siru? And the rest of the family?" I was dying to find out about Atti, but knew he'd be furious if he discovered the risks she'd taken.

As if in answer, she walked in and winked at us. "Wow— it's *really* good to see you again!" Fortunately, the adults assumed I liked her and that was why I was pleased to see her again. They had no idea that I thought she might be dead.

"I am full of joy to see you again Alek, Chimes!"

I felt myself blush. The adults noticed and were now totally convinced that there was some boy-girl thing going on between us.

Arjun coughed uncomfortably and continued, "Oh, we are well, but the Maoists have become very strong in Rajapur and everyone is getting frightened. Even poachers are scared of them. If the Maoists hear gun-shots in the jungle, they come and take away the gun!"

"The animals—the wildlife—must be safer now then? That's good."

"Maybe. The trouble is that Maoists need money, and they don't mind how they get it. Rhino horn, tiger bone, bears'

156

bile, and big cat skins fetch good prices on the black market. They get smuggled into China and places like that. No longer do I know what goes on in Rajapur. Everyone is scared—the police especially. And these days we can't even buy beer in the bazaar*."

"Bad news," Dad chuckled, clapping Arjun between the shoulder-blades. "Hard luck! Sorry I didn't bring you some."

A skinny, miserable-looking man with hunched shoulders called us into the Chief Inspector's office and then scuttled out like a spooked mongoose.

Big flakes of paint were peeling off the windows of the Big Man's office. He wasn't alone. He'd been in conversation with two other men, who turned as we walked in. One was that Tek Bahadur again. The other was Dad's field assistant. He'd survived the avalanche!

Dad said, "Ah, Ramdin. Hope you've come to help clear up a few things? Explain..."

Ramdin avoided looking at us, rose without a word, and left the room. How do Nepalis manage to look so unemotional? He hadn't looked surprised to see us. I couldn't read whether he was relieved or disappointed we weren't dead.

Dad looked hurt and bewildered. I was too. What *was* going on? Was he a Maoist—or policeman—or both? Surely he'd been our good friend once? We used to look up to him.

The big man didn't ask us to sit. He was scowling, wearing the same unfriendly expression as he did when his Toyota pickup nearly ran us down in the Chisapaani Gorge. Dad addressed the Chief Inspector politely and explained about the kidnap.

"What do you know about the men involved? What are

their names?" the policeman asked.

"I heard one man—the leader—being called *bagh*-sahib*," I said.

"Ah, The Tiger: a noble warrior—fighting against the powers of the West."

"You KNOW him!" I spluttered.

The Inspector turned to Dad, "This boy shows no respect for his elders or for the Nepali people. And my informants have told me that they have been doing things under cover. This is not how foreigners should behave in my country. Where are your passports?"

"The kidnappers took them," Dad said. He looked beaten.

"So I have to take your word—the word of an interfering foreigner—about your story and you cannot even prove who you are, or whether you have a visa to be in Nepal?"

"All our visas and permits are in order..."

"You can say this, but you can prove nothing. You admit to stealing a *dinghy* also. I think we should put you into one of our cells. I will make some enquiries."

"We paid for the canoe," I shouted, really angry now. "And we love Nepal; we're here to help."

"Help? Help who!" The Inspector turned back to Dad. "Your boy is so arrogant!"

"But..." I could see Dad trying to control his emotions. Finally, he stuttered. "May I call the British Embassy, please?"

"Maybe tomorrow. Do you have a mobile phone? No? That is a pity. Our police phones don't work well. You know how it is in *developing* countries. Nothing works. Such a pity. The lines to Kathmandu are always busy."

I had a terrible sinking feeling in my stomach, and Mum

started to cry, silently. I'd never seen her cry before.

We were bundled out of the office and down a long unlit corridor. It didn't smell good. The cell they put us in was dank and smelled worse. Two geckos on the ceiling were studying each other.

"At least we are together again!" Mum said trying to cheer everyone up.

I said, "Surely the police will have to tell the Embassy about us sometime soon?"

Mum looked miserable again.

Dad said, "I hope you're right, Alex." His voice was flat and without hope. A large cockroach ran across the floor and over my leg.

"Why did the Maoists pick on us?" I asked.

"I don't know," Dad answered. "Easy target, I suppose. Locals know that we don't carry weapons, and they'd guess that we could raise a good ransom."

I sketched out our side of the story, while Mum looked increasingly horrified.

Dad was only half listening. He said, "Hmm. I wondered who I'd upset locally. The community development work that we've been doing has shown the villagers some exciting possibilities—in the kinds of ways that the Maoists promise endlessly, but haven't delivered. So maybe I've made some dangerous enemies. I'd hate to think that is the reason, though, because these people deserve some help, they really do."

"Yeah, that really hurt when the Chief Inspector said we don't care about Nepal or Nepalis..."

"I know; I hate it too, Alexander...."

One of the geckos above us uttered his odd grinding call

and rushed at the other. The attacker clamped his toothless jaws around the body of the other gecko. They wrestled. They broke free. They locked mouths. They fell to the floor with a splat. Separated from its owner now, the tail of one writhed on the ground. Each gecko ran up different walls and became motionless again.

There were footsteps in the corridor and the sound of keys in the lock. Arjun appeared at the door and let in the boy who carried four shiny stainless-steel trays piled high with steaming rice and lentils, curried vegetables, yoghurt and lurid chutney. It smelt fantastic.

"I don't like this business," Arjun said. "This Inspector-*sahib*'s cousin is The Tiger. This creates a big problem; a very big problem. When he releases you—split up and Alek and Chimes you must run fast: run and hide. Try to get a message to your embassy. Just do this. I dare not help any more. Don't tell anyone I have spoken this way..." Looking as if he was carrying the weight of the whole world on his shoulders, he locked us in again.

"What does he mean?"

"I don't know, Alexander, but I *do* know that Arjun is a good man and I trust him. It is not easy for him—it never has been as he is lower caste than most of his colleagues. If he does anything even slightly out of line, they give him such a hard time. There's a lot going on that we don't know about, and I wouldn't be too surprised if the Maoists happen to know when we are let out and happen to bump into us again."

"Do you know anything about Tek Bahadur Rai?"

"Who?"

"The guy with the big moustache who was talking to the

Chief Inspector when we arrived in his office. We think he's doing some bad stuff."

"Ah yes. Interestingly there were some accusations about him being involved in trafficking*, but nothing's ever stuck."

"What's trafficking," James asked.

"You're too young to know, James," Mum replied.

"But..."

A team of ants had already gathered around the gecko's tail and were dragging it across the bare concrete floor. I'd seen them do this before. Their nest must be close.

Dad continued, "Arjun is right. If we could contact the Embassy—or you could contact the Embassy—then we might have some chance of rescue.... Are you listening, Alexander?"

"Yeah. Course I am."

Dad pulled a disapproving face and continued, "If we get out, we must separate immediately and you go straight to the irrigation office and ask Dinesh if he'll let you phone Kathmandu. We know we can trust him. Tell him what's going on. Mum and I'll head for the main Post Office and try to phone from there. If Arjun is wrong, and there's no Maoist reception committee, we'll meet at the Post Office and take a *tanga* to the ferry at Kothiyaghat and then the bus for Kathmandu. But enough chat. Let's enjoy this wonderful curry while it is still hot. It smells like the best I've tasted for weeks."

He was right. I put the first dollop of food into my mouth, but then stopped chewing for a moment to appreciate the flavours that spread over my tongue and got my juices flowing. There was potato and bitter gourde and cardamom and coriander and cumin and so many other great tastes. James, meanwhile, was bolting his rice down, emitting muffled *mmms* and *so goods*. He continued to swallow his food at a rate I could never manage.

I'd eaten only a couple of delicious mouthfuls when there were footsteps in the corridor. There was the sound of keys in the lock again. A new policeman entered and, indicating the plates of food, said, "This is not allowed." The skinny, miserable-looking man with hunched shoulders stepped in to take our plates away. James lunged forward to grab two more last handfuls. He stuffed one handful of rice-and-curry slop into his mouth then just managed to snatch a piece of lime chutney before the plate was out of reach. Mum, Dad and I had hardly eaten anything.

The skinny man then produced a greasy bucket with a stained enamel mug floating on an unpleasant grey fluid. He tipped small quantities into four bowls and pushed them towards us with his foot. I felt tears well up. One dropped into my bowl.

James peered into his. "Mmm. Look, they've left a grain of rice in it by mistake!"

Despite everything, he made me laugh. Then I managed, "It's not fair—tell James he has to share it with me and Mum!" We all laughed. What else could we do? James was *such* as idiot.

"You know, Alex," James said, "It's time to think of jellied eels and custard again."

Mum gave him a strange look.

"Funny how I don't feel hungry any more," she said, then added, whispering now, "I hope Arjun isn't in trouble because of us. I think being our friend is making him enemies."

Once we'd finished slurping our greasy gruel, Dad said,

"Looks like they're intending to keep us here over night, at least."

He banged on the cell door and shouted in Nepali, "Hey, brother! Any chance of some blankets?!" His voice echoed, followed by silence.

No one responded.

The oil in the cold food had reformed as slime inside my mouth. I was still hungry. We were all cold. And maybe they wouldn't even let us out in the morning. We knew people are sometimes kept locked up for ages. I didn't want to even think about how long they might keep us here. We couldn't expect to be rescued.

There was no bedding or even straw mats. It was going to be a long horrible night.

To be continued...

GLOSSARY

Nepali and other unfamiliar words highlighted in the text with *
are defined here.

Babu—child

Badmass—naughty or mischievous

Bagh—tiger in Hindi and Nepali; see animal list below.
There is a street called Bagh Bazaar in Kathmandu;
presumably a tiger was once seen there

Bahini—younger sister

Bazaar—market

Betel— leaf of the betel pepper, *Piper betle,* chewed with
the betel or areca nut, tobacco, lime, spices, etc., as paan. It
reduces hunger, so poor people chew it if they can't afford
food

Chiso—cold and **Paani**—water, so Chisapaani means "cold
water"

Dai—older brother

Didi—older sister

Dinghy—a small boat; this Hindi word has been adopted
into English to mean a sailing boat

Ganesh—the elephant-headed Hindu god of wisdom, books
and jollity

Gurkha—Nepali mercenary soldiers who are recruited into
the British Army

Haati—elephant

Himal—a mountain that always has snow on it

164

Himalaya—place of eternal snows

Howsatt—a call heard in cricket, when a batsman is caught or bowled or is otherwise thought to be out. It is a shortened version of "How is that?" as the bowling side appeals for confirmation from the umpire—the white-coated referee who stands behind the wicket at the opposite end to the batsman

Hunchha—"is"; often used like "yes"

Jelabi—deep-fried coils of crisply fried batter that have been soaked in sugar syrup. The syrup is contained inside crunchy outer layers which explode deliciously in your mouth when you bite into them

Jungle—this word has come into the English language from Hindi/Nepali. In Nepal the word means useless or wild, uncultivated land

Kaag—a crow

Kahan porio—people use this phrase on the phone to ask who is calling, but it literally means "where from?"

Karma—effect of things you have done in the past; the payback for good or bad deeds; the luck people have

Khukuri—large curved knife used as a hatchet to cut firewood and kill chickens. A weapon of Gurkha soldiers

Laddoo—ball-shaped, deep fried sweet made from flour and sugar.

Long-drop—toilet that is a simple hole in the ground. There is no water to flush it and usually no paper either

Lungi—cloth wrapped around like a sarong

Maaf—sorry

Matriarch—senior female leader of a herd

Mero—my

Pheri betaw la—until we meet again

Puja—Hindu or Buddhist prayers or a festival when people take offerings to a temple or holy place; there may be a sacrifice

Queerie—white-skinned foreigner

Rajapur—the largest of the many islands in the big rivers that come out of the Himalayan foothills; more than 100,000 people live there. Rajapur is surrounded by the largest tributary of the holy Ganges River. The main town on the island is also called Rajapur

Sahib—gentleman; term of respect for people of rank and to Westerners. It means sir or mister

Sati haru—friends

Shiva—the great god of destruction and recreation; the most powerful of the Hindu trinity

Tanga two wheeled, horse-drawn taxi; miscalled a tonga by the British during the colonial period

Tharu—caste or tribe of people who live in the low flatlands of Nepal

Topi—hat

Trafficking—taking people away to be sold into slavery

Verandah—long shaded porch along the front and/or sides of a house

NEPALI WILDLIFE MENTIONED IN THIS BOOK

Barbet—attractive small but surprisingly noisy greenish fruit-eating birds with thick beaks. One makes a sound remarkably like someone tapping metal, so it is sometimes called the coppersmith (*Megalaima haemacephala*).

Bats—both insectivorous and fruit bats live in Nepal. The little insect-hunters are almost blind but "see" by interpreting the echoes of their squeaks. Because they are small they have to find roosting places that will keep them warm while they rest during the day and they sometimes move between caves or "commute" according to the season. Fruit bats or flying foxes have excellent eyesight and can be huge. The biggest of Nepali species has a wingspan of 1.2m and is one of the largest bats in the world. They love mangoes.

Bayar—*Ziziphus mauritiana* little fruit with a stone, also known as the Chinese date or Indian plum. The fruit is sour when immature, but sweet and delicious when ripe.

Bears—two species are mentioned in the novels: the Sloth Bear (see S below) and the much larger Himalayan Black Bear (see H below).

Bee-eater—superbly coloured birds that feed on insects and nest in holes that they make in sandbanks.

"Blood-sucker" Lizard—*Calotes versicolor,* the common garden agamid or "bloodsucker" so-called because of the colour the males turn in the breeding season. They are medium-sized iguana-like lizards often about 20cm long. Sometimes they are called chisel-toothed lizards.

Brain fever bird—the Common Hawk Cuckoo, *Cuculus varius;* its very loud, crazy-sounding calls are often heard during the hot weather in the lowlands of Nepal, and in much of South Asia. It is about 34cm long.

Butcher-bird—he aggressive little bird British people call the butcher bird is the hook-billed shrike. The rufous-backed shrike, Lanius schach, is common in Nepal, and Newars kill the birds and use the beak like a little spoon at the first rice-feeding ceremony when babies take their first solid food.

Cicada—enormous noisy sap-sucking flying insects. The Asian empress cicada holds the record for being the world's loudest insect. When predators are about they sing more quietly in the hope that another cicada will be heard and eaten rather than them. They begin their lives underground feeding on root sap but then climb up the tree-trunk to "hatch" into the adult that has wings and a loud call. It is common to find empty cicada larva cases still holding onto the tree-trunk that was their nursery.

Crocodile—see mugger and gharial.

Curry leaves—the shrubby plant or small tree *Murraya koenigii* that is responsible for the idea that in the Indian sub-continent food is called curry or karri. These leaves are often added to "curries" and are also called sweet neem leaves.

Daphne—shrub that has little off-white flowers and a beautiful perfume.

Deer—see Spotted Deer.

Dog—*Cuon alpines,* the Indian Wild Dog; weighs up to 20kg and measures 55cm at the shoulder. Called the dhole in India and Nepal, a pack has been reported to have killed a tiger. Working together, they often take down prey as big as 250-kilo sambar stags and even sometimes wild buffalo.

Dolphin—*Platanista gangetica,* the 2½ metre long almost blind Gangetic dolphin; a fish-eater that finds food using sonar and never enters the sea.

Elephants—*Elephas maximus* or *haati* the so-called Indian elephant lives in Nepal and south-east Asia too. It stands about 3m at the shoulder; none of the females and only some males have tusks, whereas in Africa, elephants of both sexes have tusks. Males can weigh over five tonnes. Adults eat about 150kg of food each day.

Emerald dove—*Chalcophaps indica* the males have impressive greeny bronze wings; they are about 27cm long.

Flap-shelled mud turtles—*Lissemys punctata* which can shut up like garages. Commonly these are small animals but one weighed in at 4.5kg. They can survive without food for two years.

Flying fox—Great Indian fruit bat, *Pteropus giganteus* - see bats (above).

Gecko—the common house gecko, *Hemidactylus flaviviridis*, is flesh coloured and about 10cm long. They can shed their tails (as a defence) and regrow them, although the second version always looks stumpy and not so elegant.

Gharial—*Gavialis gangeticus*, the thin-snouted, fish-eating crocodile; not dangerous—unless you are a fish. They have a big gristly nubble on the end of the nose which helps their nostrils float just above water.

Hare—*Lepus nigricollis,* properly called the black-naped hare as it has a dark brown or black triangle from the ears down to the shoulders; it weights up to 3.6kg.

Himalayan Black Bear—*Selenarctos thibetanus* are fond of breaking into bees nests in search of honey. They are huge, the biggest measuring much as 195cm nose to rump, but when rearing up on their back legs they are even taller. They weigh up to 180kg.

Jungle Fowl—*Gallus gallus*, the wild bantam and perhaps the colourful ancestor of our farmyard chickens; they are 43-58cm long.

Kingfisher—In Nepal it is possible to see the tiny kingfisher that also lives in Europe, and there are larger species including the pied or black and white species.

Langur—*Semnopithicus entellus,* a slender light-coloured kind of leaf monkey with a long bell-pull tail. They are sociable and go around in troops of 10—35 individuals. They have complex stomachs that allow them to ferment the leaves they eat so they can get more nutrition from an otherwise poor source of food.

Leech—black worm-like creature that sucks blood; it injects anaesthetic so you can't feel the bite and also a chemical to stop the blood clotting so it can feed for hours. Leech bites therefore often bleed for hours.

Leopard—*Panthera pardus* a medium sized "big cat" that weighs up to 70kg. They are cunning solo hunters and sometimes turn man-eater. Even so they are rarely encountered in tiger country. A tiger would kill any leopard in its territory if it could.

Lizard—see "blood-sucker"; skink.

Magnolia— *Magnolia campbellii,* shrub or small tree native to the Himalayas that is now seen in gardens all over the world. They have skinny trunks but huge white cup-shaped flowers.

Mongoose—*Herpestes edwardsi,* is tawny, yellowish-grey and weighs 1.4kg and is up to 90cm long of which 45cm is tail.

Monkey, rhesus macaque—*Macaca malata,* quarrelsome, greedy temple monkey of Asia. They have short tails and weigh up to 10kg. They live in troops of 20 to 70 monkeys with a big dominant male in charge. They can carry plenty of food in their cheek pouches. They are clever and often attack if they think you are carrying food.

Mugger Crocodile—*Crocodylus palustris,* also known as the marsh crocodile, can weigh up to 200kg. Although they grow throughout their lives they rarely measure more than four metres in length.

Orb Spider—*Nephila spp.* builders of some of the largest webs in the world.

Otter—the Asian small-clawed otter, *Aonyx cinerea,* that the boys saw is smaller and more sociable than the otters we have in Europe.

Peacock—large birds related to pheasants. The male is a superb blue colour with a long tail with 'eyes' at the tip. He can raise his tail to a fan, to impress drab brown females.

Porcupine—*Hystrix indica* a large rodent whose hair has evolved into spines. When threatened they rapidly reverse into predators, the spines break off and cause infection and often death, so porcupines can kill leopards. Porcupines weigh up to 18kg.

Python—*Python molurus* a massive non-venomous snake that can measure up to 5.8m and weigh up to 90kg. They manage to gulp down porcupines, small deer and even leopards. When swallowing large prey the snake will sometimes stick its windpipe out of the corner of its mouth. Pythons can fast between meals for up to two years.

Rhino or Rhinoceros—*Rhinoceros unicornis* is the second largest of rhinoceroses, after the African white rhino. Male Great "Indian" rhinos weigh up to 2.2 tonnes and measure as much as 180cm at the shoulder. Females weigh 1.6 tons or about the same as a family car; even a newborn baby rhino weights 60kg. This species is coming back from the brink of extinction and—thanks to reintroductions—is now quite abundant in the national parks in Nepal's lowlands.

Sal Tree—*Shorea robusta* is the dominant tree of Nepal's lowland jungles. It is called an ironwood because the wood is so dense that it sinks. It is also so hard, it isn't attacked by termites so it is used for railway sleepers. The sap is used to make boats and roofs water-proof and "butter" extracted from the seeds can be used in cooking.

Salties—big aggressive salt-water or estuarine crocodiles.

Scorpion—eight-legged, armoured predators that kill their prey with venom in a stinger at the end of the tail. The sting is painful for several days and occasionally kills people.

Silk-cotton Tree—*Bombax ceiba,* gigantic trees that are propped up by huge buttresses in their trunks but which are soft enough to carve into dug-out canoes. Their seeds (in pods) are surrounded with fluffy cottony material that can be used to make lumpy uncomfortable pillows. Properly called the Indian red silk-cotton tree, its big red cabbagey flowers in appear in March. It is called *simal* in Nepali and Hindi.

Sloth Bear—*Melurus ursinus*; when the first specimens were sent back to London, the biologists who described them mistakenly assumed they used their huge curved claws for hanging upside-down in trees—like sloths. They are not related to sloths nor is their lifestyle anything like a sloth's. These bears love breaking into termites' nests to hoover up the insects inside. They have long muzzles and can flip their upper lips back to cover their noses when sucking up termites. Sloth bears are small (about 65cm at the shoulder) but powerful and weigh up to 145kg. The Nepali for bear is *balu.*

Skink—*Mabuya carinata,* small, harmless, stumpy-tailed lizard; maximum recorded length is 29cm of which 16.5 is tail. Nepalis call them *bhali mungro.*

Spotted Deer—*Axis axis* or *chital* an attractive deer rather like a fallow but with less complex antlers. They weigh up to 86kg.

Springtails aka Collembola—tiny wingless invertebrates that inhabit the soil or bat guano in caves. They have a unique "Springing organ" that allows them to leap many times their own body-length. The biggest springtails are not much more than 5-6mm long.

Stink bug—a shield-shaped flying insect with pointy piercing mouthparts. It can let off a bad smell when threatened. Stink bugs belong to the hemiptera insect family.

Tick—blood-sucking invertebrates that sit on bushes with four of their eight legs stretched out ready to catch a passing meal. They are blind but detect a meal by sensing breath, body odors, body heat, moisture, and vibrations with their front legs. Some can recognise a shadow. Their legs are barbed and they cement their mouthparts to their victims so are painful to pull off; if the mouthparts break off you can get a nasty infected bite site. Some ticks can live without feeding for up to 10 years.

Tiger—*Panthera tigris* or *bagh* in Nepali. The largest and most powerful of the big cats. They weigh up to 250kg.

Vultures—eight different species live in Nepal. In the lowlands the Indian griffon (or long-billed) vulture is common and clears up a lot of disgusting rotting flesh. In the mountains the bearded vulture or lammergeier can be seen, and there are also yellow-faced Egyptian vultures and others.

Woodpecker—there are 22 kinds in Nepal. The boys encountered the large golden backed woodpecker, *Chrysocolaptes lucidus,* which is 33cm long.

ACKNOWLEDGEMENTS

The Himalayan eco-adventures started as bedtime stories for my youngest son when he was 10 years old. He's now 21. I haven't been working on the books all that time, but they've been put to one side while I got on with my day job and also other writing for adults. During the years that I've worked on the stories, many other writers have given me help and feedback and my greatest supports have come from members of two writers' groups—in Walden Writers I have been encouraged and assisted by founder member Amy Corzine, wise kindly Victor Watson, prolific Rosemary Hayes, insightful Penny Speller and enthusiastic, encouraging Gabrielle Palmer. They have showed me how to fix places in the books where I knew the story wasn't "working" but couldn't see why.

In Cambridge Writers my biggest writing chums are the intrepid and well-travelled ladies Sally Haiselden and Françoise Hivernel, who forever tell me that my writing is transporting and funny. Many other members of the society have also helped enormously in encouraging me to complete these stories. Anyone who had tried to write knows that there are often times when confidence fails and the manuscript goes back in a bottom drawer. I am lucky that my work hasn't ever gathered much dust. I am grateful to my oldest son who has guided me on younger-generation-speak and has pointed out a few linguistic blunders. He has been consistently enthusiastic about my writing. My youngest son was an excellent critic in the early stages. Simon, too, has been quietly supportive of all my writing endeavours.

I owe Penny Eifrig a big thank you for publishing this book. She has been a delight to work with—even at great distance. I am also indebted to Betty Levene not only for her enormous talent in producing zoologically accurate drawings, but also for making these wonderful works of art too. I am so proud that she agreed to contribute to this book. Her work adorns and enhances the story.

Thank you one and all.

ABOUT THE AUTHOR AND ILLUSTRATOR

Jane Wilson-Howarth didn't find school easy because she is a bit dyslexic; but she grew up surrounded by her dad's books, and she loved his stories. She soon realised you can learn a lot from reading. She studied zoology and conservation, then parasites at university and then completed a third degree and became a medical doctor. She works as a GP (family physician) in England, treating nasty coughs and tummy aches, supporting cancer patients, doing small operations, and caring for people too ill to leave their homes.

Before that, she worked for 11 years helping people in hot countries to avoid becoming ill. She lived in Nepal for six years and has met all the animals mentioned in the books. Some came into her garden, others surprised her when she was trekking. She hopes these books show how wonderful the natural world is and will encourage readers to do all they can to help reduce global warming and stop thoughtless squandering of its precious resources.

Jane has written three books about how to stay healthy when travelling or on holiday and she has written books for adults about her life in Nepal and also about expeditions she organised to Madagascar. Her website contains lots of photographs taken in those two countries (www.wilson-howarth.com).

Betty Levene studied Fine Art at Falmouth School of Art, Cornwall, after a childhood spent in London, where she bunked off a fair bit of school in favour of wildlife watching. As an environmental campaigner, she has learned lots about the natural world and basic zoology and has undertaken wildlife and other illustration work for Jane Wilson-Howarth's Bradt & Cadogan travel guidebooks, Sussex and Cornwall Wildlife Trusts, the United Nations Association, among others, as well as for children's story illustrations. She currently lives in Cornwall where she has been supporting Bio Science university students in their studies and learned some more about animal physiognomy, teaching organic gardening, and creating traditional wooden board games.

175

CHASING THE TIGER
THE SECOND ALEX AND JAMES ECO–ADVENTURE IN NEPAL

"...the kidnappers will take your parents up to Dhorpatan. It's lawless and very remote. You can not go there..." Dinesh said.

"Why not?"

"It is too dangerous—even for well-equipped adults."

"Someone's got to go after them. It's up to us. We've got to. You know we have, Dinesh. We know what we're doing. We've been close to this area before."

"It is too difficult. We must wait for your Embassy to act. There are two high passes and very few villages offering shelter. And there are bears also. They chase people...kill some..."

Bimbini came into the room. "Really, Daddy! What are you saying? Are you trying to totally scare our friends?" She smiled a huge welcome. "Daddy, I think you are exaggerating!"

"No, Bimbini, I am not. You must just wait, boys."

My heart sank. "We can't just sit around doing nothing!"

"You are right, Alex. I have decided that you must go, and I need to go with you!" Bimbini said.

"Cool!" we both said.

"Daddy was planning to take my brothers and me on a pilgrimage to the undying flame in the mountain at Mukhtinath. He bought us back-packs and warm jackets. These will be perfect for us. I will also put *churpi* inside and biscuits and some firecrackers..."

"Err...fire-crackers. Why firecrackers?"

"They're excellent for scaring away leopards and bears—and terrorists...."

"But won't your dad be angry with you?"

"Of course," she said laughing. "He will be very angry, but only for a short time."

...COMING SOON

Lightning Source UK Ltd.
Milton Keynes UK
UKOW05f0747290117
293032UK00009B/204/P